WILLIAM JAKAB

BASA

LitPrime Solutions
21250 Hawthorne Blvd
Suite 500, Torrance, CA 90503
www.litprime.com
Phone: 1-800-981-9893

Published by LitPrime Solutions   07/28/2021

ISBN: 978-1-954886-92-6(sc)
ISBN: 978-1-954886-93-3(e)

Library of Congress Control Number: 2021915816

CONTENTS

CHAPTER 1

Basa was just a little puppy when her new master brought her home from the reeds. The moment Basa's new master, a peasant, saw the little strong looking white-as-snow puppy dog; he liked her and gave a bucket of wine to the head-shepherd---Basa's former owner. The head-shepherd looked after Basa sadly and said to the soon-to-be owner:

"This puppy is going to grow up to be a big strong dog- a good dog"

The peasant then looped a rope around the little dog's neck, tipped his hat, and within a moment, they vanished amidst the labyrinth of reeds.

Taking a deep breathe the head shepherd sighed aloud to himself,

There are as many dogs here as there are fleas. Can't use them all anyway, they're only good for hunting and prowling. Though I did feel the need for this little wine, perhaps Look-out, Basa's mother, would bare another puppy, just like Basa, in her next litter.¬

That was how Basa came to live with the Fodor Balasz peasant household.

For the first few days the Fodor Balasz family tied her up with a rope to make sure she could not cut loose and run away. A little puppy like Basa could get into a lot of trouble. Somebody could steal her, a strange dog from the reeds might bite her, or a wolf could have a meal out of her.

Stretched out like a white fur cap, Basa laid down all day at the end of this rope, looking toward the reeds which grew at the edge of the Fodor property. She listened to the swaying stalks whisper and rustle. At nightfall, when the sun went down, and everything became dark, Basa would cry and start to whimper in a low grumbling voice; she longed to be back with the rest of her family. Basa missed her brothers and sisters, and her mother Look-out. In her sleep Basa cried as she dreamt of her mother herding the sheep, leaping high, jumping left and right, keeping the herd together. Basa also dreamt of her brothers and sisters as they played around her old master; the head-shepherds' feet, tugging and nipping at the hem of his long trousers. The cold and the dark reminded Basa that she was alone without her brothers and sisters and she missed the warmth of their fur coats beside her.

In the swampy marshland of her birthplace, flocks of sheep took rest for the night. But all the new scents and never-seen-before animals at her new home: horses; cows; hens; and geese, tickled her nose. Never before had she sensed the strong unpleasant smell or felt the touch of any other human, else than the head-shepherd. Though the head-shepherd had a strong, unpleasant reek, there was a delightful ecstasy to be had amidst her brothers' and sisters' different exhalations of breath and a sheep's strong, strong, sweat steams. Here, at once, a thousand shimmering things she had never known.

The Fodor Balasz household consisted of a newly-wed couple. The man was quiet, and his stature was very tall and lean, yet his build was also very strong. He spoke little, the type of man who chose his words carefully. The peasant's strong-working arms never made any unnecessary movements. Fodor's temperament was probably the reason he never stroked or caressed Basa. Basa's new owner had strong-willed and motivated thoughts to make Basa the best watchdog. Fodor did not want to spoil her nature, the toughness of a Kuvasz's (the type of dog Basa was) over thousand year long stretch of breeding. Fodor's wife was completely different from her husband. The woman was a little chubby, and her mouth never stopped- like a brook over flowing. The heavy farm-work she had as her tasks could not kill her light, bubbly nature. Fodor's wife always found time to feed Basa, patting her on the head and stroking her behind her ears. "You little lambskin", she would say. At these times Basa felt like she was in heaven. Eventually Basa felt less homesick, especially while the woman pet her.

The reeds Basa came from, and the village her and her new owners lived in blended into each other like a foggy haze. Basa felt the inner struggle of missing the music from the reeds she once knew so well. Basa felt the reality of her present, and dealt with her past which was long-gone. As the time passed, Basa began to accustom herself to the village and she knew all the animals and peoples. Basa also worked hard. If a cow was hesitating to go into the barn, Basa drove the cow in and barked with authority. Basa also knew she was to never touch or bite the chickens in the hen-yard, but had the authorization to denounce them if they got into the vegetable garden.

As for the pigs, it was best to just grab them by the ear and pull them down to the ground, especially when they got wild and started running like mad.

In the beginning of her stay in the village, Basa had a lot of trouble with all of the other dogs there. Basa came home many times with bloody wounds all over her body and torn up skin. Even though Basa was much bigger than the treacherous neighboring spotty dog who was a real sneak, Basa often got nipped and ran home crying. Eventually, Basa's time came. Once this beautiful Kuvasz turned one and a half Spotty started a fight with Basa.. Basa lifted Spotty by the neck and into the air, shaking him until a large piece of skin was left between her teeth. With her first taste of blood, Basa became fearless and courageous. A week after Basa and Spotty's fight, Basa beat up the village's strongest dog. After that, no dog in the village would start a fight with Basa.

By the time Basa was two years old, she grew even bigger in size- she was huge- the size of a calf. The muscles of Basa's strong neck were as tight as a taught rope, her paws left hand-sized prints, and with her bare weight she was able to tip over a strong man. Basa was able to pull down a big bull and make the bull stand completely still. The peasant, her master, liked to brag that Basa was able to stop a runaway four-horse coach. This dog had smooth snow white hair around her shoulders. Basa became the ruler of the village, and was she afraid of any man or animal. She never picked a fight however, for she inherited a pleasant and peaceful nature from her shepherd mother.

Aside from her original job as a watchdog, when her masters were safe at home, Basa hunted all day in the reeds. Basa felt free in her life as a hunter. All night Basa was at home watching the house, half-asleep and half-awake- always aware. The smallest noise would wake her up. The serf, like a peasant, did not usually have fences- Basa drew her own boundaries. If anybody crossed her realm, all they would see is a white wolf-like shadow. Basa would attack an invader by flying in the air and growling in a deep tone- any man would fall down under her weight and he would experience a snarling giant dog flashing teeth at his throat. Fodor Balazs would come out with an ax, scared to death- relying on Basa's protection- when the thieves or drunks had crossed the lines Basa defended. Whoever it was, whether it be a thief or a drunk, of which there were lots in the village, Basa would watch and look at the invader, snarling, until her master would reach out his hand and patted her on the head.

"No, no, Basa. What kind of killer temper have you?"

The man who invaded the Fodor Balazs and Basa's territory started to quiver from his near death encounter. Basa's master, unlike the drunk or thief, had no reason to be afraid of his dog. When Basa opened up to somebody that somebody would stay in her heart forever, nothing could falter her tendency to love them. Any negative situation thrown upon her could not make her angry, not even the time when Fodor Balazs took away her newborn pups and drowned them in the water. For two days she had had a bursting nipple, and from morning to evening her nose was down to the ground looking for what was left of the scent on the riverbed, before her pups were tossed into the water.

The first time Fodor Balazs killed four out of five of Basa's pups, Fodor's wife asked him,

"Why are you killing those harmless, innocent pups? Do you have any heart? What harm have they done to you?"

It was like a mother's heartfelt grief and a tear drop began to flow down her cheek. Basa sensed the sensitivity in Fodor's wife's voice. Fodor responded reluctantly,

"The pups would make her weak, sucking away all her energy"

"Ah, good man! Are you really worried about your dog or do you just want to make sure you are able to brag about her again and again?" You would not care if all this work killed me." The wife was getting older while Basa had a square, lean, body. While Fodor's wife pet Basa on the head she uttered, "I am aging five years after just one year passes. Even when I was a pretty girl, you never bragged about me".

This was not the only fight the couple had on account of Basa, but Basa had a strong feeling about the complaints of the woman- this fight was not about the woman but really about Basa's pups. The murder of Basa's pups is what was making the woman upset. Basa understood a lot about human affairs, more than the people around her knew. From that moment on, after the wife defended her, the wife grew nearer to Basa's heart, even if the woman did not care about Basa as much as she cared for her own children who were being born one after another. A lot of work and a heavy burden came with the birth of her children. Regardless, Basa's master was Fodor Balazs. Fodor barely fawned over Basa, but to her he was a man-god, quiet and silent. He rarely gave a pat on the back. But, he was the one Basa would give her life for if the time came, and next in rank were their children.

From the moment they were able to come to the yard, crawling toward her, they had made their imprint on Basa. Basa would lie down next to the kids in the dust; her great beautiful head resting on her first two paws, watching them so they did not get into trouble and so strangers would not get too close.

Oh, the children, the little man-gods were so helpless and awkward, Basa allowed the children to pull her white coat and hit her on the head. Basa even allowed them to get on her back and play horse. Basa was a babysitter and a toy to the kids. Oh, those little high-pitched voices, those little limbs and hands, dirty and warm bodies; they were heavenly angels to Basa, as she lay down between them, a fairy-tale genie herself, always helping them- protecting them. Basa coveted the time spent with her master's children. Basa loved to play with the children. Basa was allowed to take care of them, holding back her passion for hunting. The gentle dog loved them and she was happy to be around the Man-Gods little kids.

Basa went to hunt in the reeds less and less as the time passed. Most of the time she spent lying down at home, and she became a quiet, comfortable dog. In her prime at four years old, Basa spent time with the only pup she had left. Basa felt on top, she was really happy. Basa hoped her life would never change, and it seemed like it would never. One day, without any warning, all her happiness and everything else came to an end. At the height of summer, when the clouds were white as a goose swimming high in the sky with powerful rays of sunshine drying everything, not the smallest sigh of wind on the horizon- not helpful against quenching thirst; Basa was lying down in the shade sleeping, with her tongue halfway hanging out. At once, Basa heard lots of noise coming from the edge of the village. A great number of people on horseback were advancing toward the house. Basa's nose was hit with an unfamiliar smell that she instinctually hated.

Basa's hair had bristled up and she started growling in a low menacing voice. Fodor Balazs heard Basa make a sound and came out from the house. "Germans!" said Fodor with fear when he saw the strangers. The Germans soon reached the Fodor household, and Basa felt the danger within every bone of her body. Basa laid still and quiet. As a dog, it was not her business to interfere with peoples dealings. However, Basa did not take her watchful eyes off the loud-speaking strangers for even a second.

Fodor Balazs spoke with the haughty and arrogant foreigners. With Basa's sensitive nose, she sensed her master's fright. Basa could not fathom what her master was afraid of. The two of them could fight that many people and the horses were harmless. One of the officers struck her master forcefully in the face. Basa gave a growl and with her full-size body, weight, and wolf like muscle leapt forward like a white shadow to the throat of the stranger.

The German fell to the ground, and he was trying to protect himself with his forearm, but Basa, with her powerful jaw, broke the man's arm. It sounded like a broken twig. Basa heard her master's voice crying "Basa…Basa…", but Basa did not care anymore. Basa's nose was terribly bothered by the strange people's sour smell, her eyes were like a blazing fire, and her tongue tasted the salt of human blood.

The soldiers became terrified by the mad and frenzied wild beast as she jumped on them like white flaming darts. The soldiers were scattered all over the yard. The attacked man was pleading for help, trying to wriggle himself out from under the dog's weight. The man pushed her, the huge white-toothed demon, away from his throat with his unharmed hand. On his chest the uniform he wore was shredded from Basa's strong paw nails. Finally, one of the other soldiers snapped out of his paralyzed state and brought his rifle with him. Basa was unaware of the danger that was coming; she did not realize a rifle was coming her way and was preoccupied with the man who had hit her master.

The German soldier who was coming to the attacked man's rescue was ready to shoot his rifle. Basa was about to die and would not have been able to escape her fate, but then the captain of the soldiers arrived. Captain Stipek's had somewhat of a love affair with dogs of all kinds, for he did not have a wife and child at home- only a pack of bloodthirsty beasts. In one second, Stipek's heart warmed up to the raving huge white Kuvasz. Never before had he had in his sights a beautiful dog, a dog as beautiful as Basa. The captain knocked the rifle's barrel away and said straight-faced, "I want her alive." The soldiers took that as an order. Nobody moved.

The soldiers were murmuring to themselves. Nobody dared to poke the wild beast. Basa had already stopped biting and chewing at the unlucky officer, her victim. Basa had her head up, listening. The German officer underneath her was quiet, and he was in no condition to move. The other soldiers could not refuse the captain's order. The men surrounded Basa in a half circle, standing reluctantly and moving forward towards the white dog.

Basa was not afraid and menacingly snarled at them, like a wolf, she was protecting her prey. The strangers neared toward her slowly, and the circle was closing in on her. The only way out for Basa was through the reeds. There was an open gap between the soldiers. Though, Basa did not want to leave. Basa had an immense anger inside her that made her whole body shake. Like an arrow in mid-air, Basa was flying, shooting up at the soldiers. The soldiers were ready for her and jumped aside. Basa was jumping left to right, like she was trying to catch a fly. Basa's teeth clapped at the emptiness when she missed her target, but when she caught whiff of a bone and the warm blood dripped down her mouth, she became more ferocious. Everything in front of Basa became like a red fog. Basa lost her temper, and her anger grew into rage. The soldiers pulled out their swords for their own protection against Basa, but she still jumped at them until the sharp blade made her cool down. Basa licked her wounded shoulder and was still growling at the soldiers and their swords. Man and animal began to look at one another. "Huh, what a killer you are, "said Captain Stipek with a laugh. The captain decided he would take Basa as his own, for he had never owned such a beautiful dog. Everybody in his neighborhood would come around to look at her splendidness.

"All of you are damned like sheep", the captain said to his soldiers. "Throw a cloak over her head, idiots!" Before she had the cloak thrown over her head, Basa saw an iron sword lowering and disappearing. Basa had free reign again to attack the stranger's body. Basa jumped up at once. Afterwards, some thick cloak fell over her nose. Basa bit it, but no soldier was in it and tried to free herself. Basa got even more entangled.

Now, the soldiers were throwing the cloak on her back and jumping at her. They lowered her to the ground squeezing her with force. Basa fought back, throwing her body up and down, but the soldiers grabbed her legs and forced them together, the captain took the cloth off from Basa's head. Basa tried to catapult herself up in the air and was ready to bite the officer, but her legs were unable to help her. Captain Stipek pulled away from her snarling white teeth, and with the knowledge of a professional dog-handler, hit Basa's nose fast and hard. Basa's eyes were filled with tears and her nose began to ache. Not until that day had anybody hit her in a cruel manner. Still, Basa did not give up the fight, trying again to catapult herself in the air, but she just lay down like a drowning fish laying on the riverbank.

Captain Stipek was laughing at her. Basa tried to bite his quick and sure hand three more times, but the captain's hand was faster and surer every time. Basa's nose ached, and she was exhausted, worn out, and lying down. The fight was over. Basa had given up; she had just learned what it was like to be afraid of something.

Captain Stipek thought he had been successful at breaking the spirit of the beautiful and shaggy wild beast. The captain ordered, "Take off the cloak." When Basa felt the breeze against her body, she started up again with anger, and she was biting at her shoulder in an impotent rage. Captain Stipek was scared that this beautiful white devil had become mad, so he ordered to throw a bucket of water on the nearly insane dog. The soldiers tied a rope around Basa's mouth and, they carried her to the roadside in her weak state- drenched. Basa's beautiful white coat was covered in mud and dust. In her mind she already knew she had lost. Basa lost everything she had ever loved and whatever had been close to her heart. Basa's anger completely vanished as she lied half dead. Basa's eyes were closed and she waited until the course of events was about to end. Basa's nose ached terribly again, and her whole body shook in the hot summer's heat. Basa's eyes stayed closed as the loud screaming and smoke came from her master's house. Basa could smell her master's blood burning. Even with closed eyes, Basa knew that they killed the children, the little man gods, one by one, and then the mother and wife. Basa knew by the slowly disappearing scent of her people, exactly where they laid in the yard, and her own pup was there too with the whole family.

Basa could not move her legs, they became stiff and numb from the tight rope tied around her mouth. Basa was in anguish holding a sinking heart awaiting her own death. Basa only opened her eyes when the horrible smelling strangers, who had this hateful smell she could not stand, lifted her and put her on the wagon. Basa looked once more at the burned down house and the dead people in the yard. Basa fell down with a thud at the bottom of the wagon when they started to ride with a clatter and a shake where she could no longer see anything more than the old beat up wagon's rotten side plank. The soldiers took her away from the village. Basa could not care less, for she had nothing left anymore.

The captain of Basa's car ordered a dark-haired man by the name of Johan, with a dark and skinny appearance, to let Basa's rope loose and put meat and water in front of her. The man had some knowledge about dogs, for during his adolescence he was a dog handler for the Hungarian squire. Without fear, the dark and skinny man quickly hit Basa on the nose as she tried to bite the man's hand. Once again, the anger in the dog came to life. But, with her tightened legs, Basa felt so helpless that her head fell to the floor of the wagon with another thud. Basa did not touch any of the water or food. Basa was thirsty until the evening, refusing to drink. Basa's dried out tongue was covered with dust, and her sense of smell was lost in the dry heat. In the evening of her thirst, the captain ordered the soldiers to let Basa's legs loose before any permanent damage from the numbness could be done. At first, Basa did not want to stand, but Johan poked her until Basa stood up with numb and shaky legs. By that time, the small skinny German, tied a tricky knot around her neck that when pulled would tighten around Basa's neck until it choked her.

Basa soon realized that she did not want to fight anymore; she only wanted to drink some water. Johan saw Basa's calm demeanor. "Oh, you king of devils", said Johan, patting her all over. Basa let him touch her with detest and disgust, as she was half dead from the tantrum and pestering torment. Basa did not have the strength to fight anymore or the cunning demeanor to disguise how she was truly feeling. Basa had given up her freedom and her pride, which had been the fuel for her strength to fight on. Basa had lost her strength and her power. Walking next to Johan with obedience, Basa's legs started to come to life as they walked; she could only reach Johan's waist if she were to attempt to stand. When Basa got to the water and decided to drink, she drank with voracity. Basa was obedient except for being unaccepting of any food they gave to her. Basa and the man walked up and down in the camp between the soldiers. As she walked, Basa felt her strength come back to her. Basa felt better minute by minute. After her experience at her master's house, Basa had learned she was unable to fight so many men by herself. Instinctually, Basa knew she did not want to stay with these people. They had killed her master. Basa was mixed with feelings of fear she had never known before, and her memories as a free and wild beast.

Basa played along with the situation at hand and walked tamely next to him, gentle as a lamb. Johan was happy with his work. Johan thought the dog was easily giving in to him, and he walked Basa between the camping soldiers, back and forth. They walked all the way to the last sentry. By that time Johan felt confident with the dog, he was too sure of himself and took the rope off of Basa's neck and started petting her.

Basa's nose caught the smell of the reeds: all the different bird calls, the humidity, the cool green colors, and the smell of fish. Like a wild one jumping on prey, Basa jumped free into the dark night. Basa's powerful neck pulled away Johan's arm and Basa ran, running into the dark night and the protection of the wilderness she already knew so well.

CHAPTER 2

Basa came out of the reeds at the village's end. Maybe Basa had been mistaken after all, and the Germans did not kill her master and his family. Basa was unsure due to her weak memory of the horrible and weakened state she had been in at the time. Basa could not decipher the real truth. Basa's instinct was urging her to go back to the master's household.

The tart, bitter smell of smoke woke up her memory. Within the reeds she had already sensed the burned patches of reeds here and there. Luckily the puddle in which the hemp grew stopped the reeds fire. Basa walked through the burned ash; her beautiful white hair and coat got dirty from black flakes of soot. The house stood just the way the Germans had left it.

Basa smelled the cold smell of dead corpses. In the ruins of the house, one man, who had escaped the German's ravage stumbled around while he went fishing in the reeds. Just before, the man had been rummaging through the ruins. The escapee was covered in black soot, like Basa was. On his face the tears fell and the soot was cleaned away, shining in streaks. For a moment, the escapee was scared of the dog's crying; he wanted to run, but he calmed down and slowly approached Basa. "Come over here," he called to her with a friendly invitation, patting his knee with his open hand. Basa stopped her wolfish cry and like a wild beast that had never been around the sound of a human, she showed the huge white teeth in her mouth. All of a sudden, she ran back into the reeds. Basa did not want to go backward and stay with any human anymore. Basa's master was dead, and so was the rest of his family. All of them had died from human hands.

Although, Basa, had learned a long time ago that she could not figure out the logic of humankind, not as easily as she knew the way of the dog. Basa either wanted to find prey, or she wanted to sleep now that she was cold.

No, the human way is much more complicated than the way of the dog. You cannot see through their senseless, pointless killing. It is madness, like a bloodthirsty scoundrel who finds its way into the sheep heard and is going to kill thirty or forty sheep, when only one would be enough to fill the hunger.

Basa's clear thinking would not take another risk when it came to humans. And so, her fate was to turn away from humankind altogether.

Basa took one sniff of the air. Now her life depended on her hunting skills and instinct. Basa was already familiar with the animals in the reeds. Basa had met with them many times in her private hunting trips of the past. At that time, it had only been for play- a game. Now, Basa's life depended on how successful she would be at catching her prey to survive.

The space of the reeds was loud from all the different early-birds songs. The slightest breeze brought about a thousand scents. Basa was hungry. Cautiously and stealthily, from one marshy bog to another, she got closer to the open water where all the water-birds were playing. Basa's tail was up, as was customary for all Kuvaszs'. The birds Basa was hunting flew after her when she attacked. She was peering out from the reeds and prowling for a hunt.

The once glittering water was blackened from the thousands of water-birds. Some from the big group were roused, startled, and flew up into the sky. Their feet and wings made a sound like the rolling sea. On the surface of the countless duck regiments melting together was one beautiful blue-green-and gold feathered drake, swimming around carefree near the water's shore. The duck was playing and ducking under the water every second, and the water dripped down the duck's shiny feathers like pearls once it came up from hunting. The carefree drake called for the other ducks that were swimming in the open water.

Basa's eyes became like hot iron as she focused at the many swimming prey in front of her. There were so many of them that they almost covered the entirety of the water's surface. Here, there was no need for Basa to choose, all she had to do was pick one and jump between them to catch a couple. Basa jumped into the thick of the birds.

The carefree duck specimens disappeared in the blink of an eye. One or two of the ducks touched Basa's side from underneath the water. The dog bit into the water. Basa went under then came up snorting. The drake, not far away, swam like nothing happened; only its big shiny eyes were blinking at the big, clumsy, white animal.

Basa already knew about the laws of the reeds; you cannot pursue a prey in an unfamiliar element. Basa was very annoyed by it as she climbed out of the water and shook the cool droplets out from her shaggy hair, and then she sat down on one of the marshy bogs to dry and watch the duck specimens. Basa had to learn new laws: her bowels were not to make a sound when hunting for prey, and she had to pick one duck and stay close to it.

The ducks soon got used to the big white motionless something and then came close swimming by. Basa's lips were trembling, eyes glowing, but she did not move. Again, the pompous, blue-green-headed drake made a curious move and swam closer. The reeds quivered and a drake tried to escape, going underwater, but a huge mouth- with teeth like a bear trap- closed on the drake's body, whose wings flapped a couple of times before it was finished off.

Basa was spitting out water and feathers as she put her prey down on the water bank. Finding a den was easy for her. Basa knew, from her earlier hunting, about a thick and dense willow-wood island. A very old willow tree rose above the bushy scrubs. The old tree's thick roots ran above the ground and, in a way, offered Basa a small den. The den belonged to one otter that lived there for some time, but looking at Basa's size, it hurried away and gave up the den, happy to be able to escape into the water.

With a little extra work, Basa dug out space to make it big enough for her to fit inside. This space became her lair. The den would be the starting point for her hunting, and at the end she would also come back. Within two weeks, Basa learned more about the laws of the reeds than she had learned throughout her entire life, hunting just for fun.

In order to catch the wild ducks, Basa had to go to the flat busy growth on the open water. Basa came upon the fact that the ducks did not have much brains- dull witted, but wide awake. If Basa went on time for the hunt, sooner or later she could catch something. If Basa was late for the hunt, it did not matter how silent Basa remained, the ducks would become aware of her. Basa discovered other parts of the reeds where the water was not deep. When this region of the waters dried up, she could catch big fishes out of the mud. In the hot summer, the water disappeared and left behind presents for the otter, fox, and all the birds. Basa learned how to hunt in the thick of the reeds; she could follow the scent of prey on leaves but not on the marshy bag. There, the prey was too far away and the water hid their scent. Once, carrying a deep wound, she learned not to hunt for stork. The sharp beak left a mark on her, and the meat was not good; it tasted bad. Basa met with all kinds of animals; she grew familiar with the voice of the bullfrogs of the bog. Once, she saw a wolf's long lean body, and one other time she attacked a young deer buck while he was drinking water, but the young deer buck was not afraid; his horns were very strong, looking straight down against the dog. Basa was afraid to jump on him, they were looking at each other, and the dog walked away.

In her body size, Basa had lost some weight. Though Basa's muscles became strong, and her sense of smell and hearing also became very sensitive. Basa's beautiful hair got tangled up and raveled; it had become a dirty white. Basa was now a real hunting predator, the strongest one in the reeds. Sometimes at evening, the smell of smoke came through the wind from far away. When that happened, Basa went to lie down in her den and cried low, just like when she was a puppy. However, Basa would not move at these times, her body tight and strong. Basa was able to fight off all the senses that flooded back to her about her humans and the smell of smoke.

As time passed, the hot summer came. One morning Basa found that the day was getting colder than before and the night was longer. Even though the seasons were changing, the humans, unlike Basa, would not realize the presence of the still hot summer heat sending you into the protective shade, but autumn was coming right around the corner. Basa's sensitive instinct felt something more than just the summer that the humans felt. Basa roamed aimlessly into the reeds and waters. She was hunting less, and her nose looked for new unrecognizable scents. Basa was longing for a mate, a dog partner.

Basa already knew that if she followed the faint smell of smoke in the air, she could find some human. In addition, where there was a human, there would definitely be some dogs around the man. Sometimes, when the sun went down, Basa would slip away to check what the humans were doing. Basa's cowardice averted her from the humans and she would only circle around them, that is, until the smell of one particular human hit her nose, and she saw the sheepherders black clothing. Nevertheless, Basa became weak within her, turned back, and ran away as if somebody had chased her until she reached the den of the island.

One looming August evening, Basa started her hunting late. The light cast a veil over the thick reeds, and far away--- a thin stream of smoke oozed up into the dark night and into the sky. The reeds' soft low whisper and buzzing was like a giant beehive where there were thousands and thousands of busy bees flying in and out to work all day. For a moment, all the water birds stopped, and with more noise than before, they went to rest for the night.

In the big lake's open water, lots of swans were swimming, and they looked like they mirrored the fleecy clouds above them. Near and far, thousands of water birds of all kinds of variations- rattling duck, gypsy duck, and many other variations- flew up and down on the water. A common coot was unaccounted for.

Near Basa, egrets picked out fish from the shallow water. Basa never hunted the enchanting egrets, for their sparkling beautiful white feathers gave her a panic stricken feeling. As it was right now, Basa just looked at them for a moment and stealthily moved away. And in a moment, one of the egrets stiffened up and gave a sign, and a silver-looking bird with a few slow wing flaps soared away into the sky. Similarly, if a fire were to break out, all the birds would surely start rattling noisily. Basa became flat as she lay down, something was coming. The predator of the reeds must know all the signs to be able to survive. It must have been a wild animal on the hunt. Across from Basa, the reeds opened and a big gray head pushed through the reeds, and the giant shoulder of a male wolf approached. The wolf was darker than the regular reddish wolf of the reeds, and his body was much bigger. He was as tall as Basa, but thinner and lighter. The old experienced solitary hunter came through the currents of wind and noticed the dog, Basa. The wolf's ears became flat, and from his throat, a short growl came out. Basa came up to a full stance. It was in Basa's blood, for the wolf was her ancient enemy, and she would have to fight until the end. But at the same time, Basa felt as if he was a family member, crossbred, and all her body told her she had found a partner in him.

Basa was not afraid of any animal. Basa was ready for a fight, but somehow did not feel the urgency of the fight. Basa's tail was up in the air, like all Kuvasz, and she was showing her giant teeth while she approached the wolf. In the meantime, Basa gave out a growl that sounded peaceful. The hair on the big grey wolf's neck became like a porcupine protecting itself from an attack, bristling. The wolf had killed a lot of dogs already, but Basa here was much bigger and stronger looking than he, and she did not have any human smell on her. If the wolf were to start a fight with Basa, one of them would surely die. As the wolf sniffed Basa's scent, something stirred inside of him- some strange feeling, the distrust of a blooming friendship. Somehow the wolf's strong and aggressive feelings toward Basa became weak, and he felt some attraction pop up- he was drawn to Basa.

Basa drew nearer to him in small steps, and with tightened muscles was ready to jump if the attack came. Basa's giant teeth clapped together. Finally Basa came close to the rigidly standing wolf. Their noses almost touched. Within a moment, the wolf, in a playful manner tried to nip Basa's nose and gave up a friendly growl. And without any hesitation, they started running together to the open pasture.

The lonely big hunter- the grey wolf- became the father of Basa's litter. For a while, he was around and hunting in the reeds, but when the yellow colors of autumn showed up and Basa's litter was born, the big gray wolf disappeared into the reeds.

CHAPTER 3

IN THE REEDS

The old male deer sniffed the air with suspicion. He was afraid to put his head down to eat the fading grass. The deer's most beautiful antlers were like two leafless boughs standing out from the dying reeds just before the winter came. He was an old buck with giant antlers and a body full of scars that showed he was a fighter who had learned how to survive. Even his hair became his eyes and ears, sensing everything. Experience taught him to be suspicious and cautious, equally important as eating, in order to live a long life.

The buck's suspicion was there only as a way to avoid wolves and a shepherd-dogs teeth or a human rifle. In moments of suspicion he could not see anything, just sense some strange eeriness from the small island. The wind coming from his back was not helping the situation. The old buck's nose became numb, but his instinct did not allow him to graze peacefully. At the island under the giant willow tree, something moved. The buck uttered a deep belch and jumped. When the buck looked back, he saw what looked like a wolf-pup crawling out from the slippery dust-and-earth mixed den. From that moment, the buck ran without stopping because where there was a small wolf, a big wolf was not far behind them.

The four puppy dogs crawled out of the den and whimpered and sniffed the weak late-fall sunshine. On the pups thick short legs they were moving clumsily, gangling around without looking. The pups hit each other and would fall down, turning over on their soft bodies in the grass. Around their neck and fat shoulders there was thick skin wrinkled with their stubby noses sniffing the grass and dust. Their little eyes had just opened up, for they were only couple-of-weeks old newborn puppies. Three of the puppies looked the same, their thick and white body hair was tousled, and they were real Kuvasz puppies.

"Little Sheepskins", Mrs. Fodor would say, like she said it before to their mother. The fourth pup had short gray hair and long legs and looked more like a wolf. For a while, they played, and the smallest "sheepskin" started whimpering and crying. All of the pups were hungry, and for them, the only important thing was to eat. Their mother, Basa, already had left a long time ago and now they did not know what happened to her. Why had she not come back yet?

The pups were waiting impatiently and demanded their mother's swollen sweet udder. First the gray puppy wolf got bored and started to cry. Outside it was cold, so it was better to climb back to the den, curl up together, and fall asleep. The other pups were still singing, they sang a little more, and the two of the white sheepskins played together, then they all got on top of each other and fell asleep on the bed of grass.

Basa sat for a long time in her hunting position until she was able to catch a coot that a fox had already crippled, and that was why it could not fly with the others to the zone of their autumn migration. The coot was a very small bite to eat for a big animal like Basa, but she was afraid to leave the pups alone for a long time. Something could happen to the pups when they were alone in the den.

With great wide jumps breaking through the reeds, the coot hung in Basa's mouth. At the edge of the island, Basa stopped and sniffed around to try to catch the scent that belonged to a dangerous animal or human.

Only the old deer buck's cold scent stayed amidst the plants, and with a relaxed thought, Basa broke through the circle of willow bushes, and with a low voice called out to her pups. In an instant, the puppies swarmed out pushing and crawling over the others. Basa did not even have time to put down the coot. The pups ran over her, and Basa almost lost her footing. Up front, the little gray one got the best nipple. Basa pushed it aside, but the little puppy- flexing legs and grabbing and biting a nipple pulled back again. All the time, the mother-Basa- was tortured with the aggressive sucking and hard biting.

Finally all of them had found a milky haven. The smallest one got a breast at the end where the nipple had less milk, but the small meaty nipple lasted many times. The runt would cry to get it back. The runt of the litter never got a good enough spot with her brothers and sisters constantly pushing her out of the way. Basa was already exhausted once she had caught the coot. Basa became very lean, almost emaciated. Basa's puppies took away all her strength. Basa did not have enough time to get meat to keep up her big body. In her weakness, the prey, the hunted animals, had an easier time escaping. With Basa's failed attempts at hunting, she got pushed to the brink of taking a big risk. Basa lost her sense of security and self-confidence.

Just a couple of days before, Basa was chasing after a big young hare to corner it. Basa could already taste the young flesh in her mouth when the hare flew over her like a jumper from the circus. The dog just looked after it with a dumb feeling. The other day Basa was attacking a two-hundred pound cat fish in the open waters, Basa could finally thank herself and her quickness that the big catfish did not pull her down underwater and that the hunter did not become the prey.

Even the birds became less frequent. You could only see them sometimes- a late migration of the flock-and you could only hear them from the far distance with their loud shouting above the yellow dying reeds. The reeds became almost lifeless. The once full table of food grew less and less every day. The hungry puppies became full, and with sleepy eyes, went stumbling back into the den.

Finally Basa was able to eat the cold coot. Basa finished it quickly: bones, head, and legs. Basa ate everything after cleaning away the coot feathers under the dry fallen leaves and parched grass. Basa never left her prey open and rotting away because the smell of the rot would reveal her secret place. The smell would invite the wolf and the fox when she was out hunting for food. With small puppies like the one's she had, even a skunk could hurt them.

Basa was still hungry. The coot was not enough to take away her great hunger. Basa went to see the puppies in the den. They were in a deep sleep. One of the little puppies made a growl and with a tiny voice made a yap. It had been a long time since Basa watched over her puppies, one of them would fight or hunt all the time in their dreams, but she was never able to see whose mouth let out the hints of a troubled dream. Basa looked back uneasily and worriedly when she left the island.

Instilled with the hope that nothing would happen to the puppies while she was away for the hunt, Basa lowered herself into the cold water and started swimming like a dog, with her head up until she reached the shore where she quickly shook the water out from her thick hair. And Basa started to run so the cold fall evening would not make her body stiff, from the heat she gathered by moving with speed. Basa already knew all the waters because in the meadows it was very rare to find a dry route. Everywhere there was a brook or stream that would change back to being dry again. But the water took up more space than the dry land. Basa had no chance. Basa had to take with a friendly gesture what nature had to offer.

Now when Basa ran after her prey, no bird was there to run or fly away. It was already autumn season. On the waters, you could no longer hear the splashes of carps playing and throwing themselves in the air. Hungry for prey, only the pikes remained for Basa, lurking and waiting. It was a heavy time for the hunters, sometimes only the bullfrogs could be found; which was only an appetizer for a big dog like Basa. But even the bullfrogs became less and less, hiding under the warm mud through the winter. Looking for prey and sniffing the reeds, Basa could run for days between the reeds without catching even a thing.

On her way, Basa got closer to the big lowlands where the herdsman's campfires showed the lights at night. At once the entire reeds were filled with smoke and the smell of humans. The flickering lights swirled around and where they did not reach, it looked like the night got thicker and darker.

Basa ventured out to the beginnings of the lowland against

the wind so that the shepherd dogs could not catch her scent. The rigorous shepherds sat in front of the hut around the fire. Basa was overcome with an overwhelming feeling, remembering the picture of how she used to be a puppy and the familiar scent of the fire and the herdsman.

Basa wanted to go near the fire and lie down submissively at the feet of the greasy-black-clothe-wearing humans and wait for a piece of the meat already warming in the pot to be thrown at her. With her whole body stretched out, Basa lay down with her nose in the grass. In the sheep- pen behind the extension of the house, the long-haired sheep grew restless and started moving quietly. The humans' shepherd dogs nose caught whiff a scent, and Basa knew this because one of them barked uncertainly, running back to the sheep-pen, trying to catch a scent- but unsuccessfully, and went back to the fire. The other dogs could not smell Basa, because she came against the wind.

"What happened with you? Did you smell a wolf?" said one of the shepherds, and, with a boot, gave a friendly kick to the dog. Basa broke away from the magic memories of her past and stood up. Basa needed to eat and hurry back to her pups. Basa realized that now she was a hunter, a wild animal.

With stealthy precaution, Basa reached the sheep-pen and jumped over the dry reed fence. The dull-witted sheep did not get scared. The sheep did not make any noise or thump the earth---they only stirred around. Nevertheless, this movement was enough for the shepherd dogs, and with wild barking; they ran toward the sheep. Basa grabbed a young lamb, and with one move of her strong giant neck, put the lamb on the back of her shoulder and fled away. Basa's mouth was filled with the lamb's long wooly hair, and though her throat was irritated, she rushed headlong ---choking.

Even with the lamb's weight, she was still running faster than the sheepdogs, but they were close behind, barking furiously and grasping at her tail. Checking on the big hubbub, the sheepherders jumped up grabbing the long lead stick and a short long whip and ran after the dogs in pursuit. One sheepherder saw the thief's white body in the dark and threw his ornamented stick at Basa. The stick almost knocked the lamb out of Basa's mouth. "Stop!" one of the sheepherders cried out grabbing his partner's arm. "The white wolf!" and the shepherd made a crucifix sign. "Go away!" he screamed after Basa. "That was a dog", he mumbled, with a shaky voice. However, he stopped, and later added, "I hope it is not only bringing us trouble because I threw a stick after it." The shepherds whistled their dogs back. "Better not start with a white wolf, because if it is not a wolf, it is a shaman in the body of a wolf. And for revenge, it can ruin or kill you." The men walked back to the head-shepherd.

Basa was losing her strength very quickly at this point, almost dropping the death-ridden lamb. The dogs were nearing, she thought. Ready to drop her prey, escape with her life, she heard a whistle and the dogs reluctantly faded away, except one who still chased her. But when Basa put down her lamb and turned to the dog, it quickly stopped and stumbled away in shambles.

Basa still could not figure out what magic played the trick for her easy escape. But, she did not care. The sound of the sheepherders whistle, like a soft milky thread, only left her mind once she jumped into the cold water. On the other side of where she swam, Basa killed the lamb and carried it away. Basa could not bring the lamb to the den, because the scent and reminder of the kill could bring trouble and lead to catastrophe.

Basa was going back to the den in a roundabout way, within the never-ending reeds' unknown parts. In the yellow reeds, Basa found a nice small island with a few willow trees and on top of a little hill was an abandoned shepherd's hut that was still in good condition. Examining the scent, no human had been around here for years. Even still, Basa went around the hut with caution and stealth to look for strange new scents. When Basa did not find anything, she became relaxed and ate the lamb. Basa buried the leftovers, hiding them in the ground, so she could have a meal for the next few days.

Afterwards, Basa hurried back to her puppies that were already hungry and waiting for her to arrive back to them. Sometimes when she could not find food for herself, she took a tithe out of the sheep flock. The sheepherders were afraid to chase her because they were superstitious of the white wolf's evil that could possibly put a curse or a magical spell on them.

Basa always traveled to eat from the sheepherders flocks at night time. The sheepherders only saw the giant white animal running away with their lamb. The shepherds did not even think Basa could be a dog, and even if they thought that it could be a dog, they were still thinking about the same magic shaman's true colors changing into a wolf. This road Basa occasionally chose was heart shaking for Basa all the time. Basa had learned that such men were very powerful and would find a way to punish her. The reeds are where she was looking for food to fuel her body.

Basa's puppies were growing and getting stronger on their mother's milk. The puppies hardly fit into the willow-tree den anymore. At night, Basa had to stay outside in front of the den, and though the night was chilly, Basa was afraid to move the puppies out into the unknown. In the late autumn the rain came almost every day. Everything was wet and muddy. The meadow's daytime became dim, and the earth was moist and damp even in the willow tree's roots. The rain dripped down into the den.

One morning, Basa woke up by the water and was washing her paws. The dirty water crept into the den, and her puppies came out, shaking and whimpering. The strong wind made the rain feel like a sharp blade. A muddy, dirty yellow wave of water came at the dogs with rumbling reeds mixed in, atop of the water. One scared bird above shouted from far away. The waves slowly took over the small island. To stay here would be the end.

Basa ran up and down at the edge of the water line. Basa was trying to look ahead, to look out, but in the heavy thick rain, she could only see the nearest wall of reeds and bushes. Basa felt the danger and was forced to flee; she carefully grabbed her smallest puppy with her teeth and started to go. The pup was obedient, and like a lifeless body, hung in her mother's mouth until the others stubbornly clung in her thick hair. Basa shook them off and started swimming without knowing where.

Basa was holding her head up high; her strong, muscular neck was becoming tired from holding her puppy high above the water. However, the oncoming waves still splashed over Basa's head, and the little puppy dog's velvety hair became wet and heavy. Basa's neck started aching from the constancy of holding her up.

Basa was swimming and swimming against the wind, but still she had not reached the shore where she would usually get out. Here, the water was everywhere. In addition, in an enlightened moment, Basa came to remember her latest discovery of that abandoned sheepherder's hut where she buried her first lamb. Basa turned back now, swimming with the waves against her, back toward the hut. The island where the sheepherder's hut stood was above water level. The flood took up a small piece of the island, but the middle remained untouched.

Basa, with her shaking legs, climbed up to the shore and let her pup down into the hut and hurried back for the rest of her family. Without any trouble, Basa brought over a second puppy. When Basa went for the third, which was the little gray wolf, her legs were trembling already. Basa could not shake all the water out of her fur well enough, and it became heavy like led, pulling her down to the bottom of the water. The little gray one was the biggest and heaviest pup she had. Basa grabbed it by the neck, but the gray one was stubborn and with flexed legs, did not want to move out from the den. The gray little wolf child was afraid of the water and at all costs, wanted to go back underneath the willow tree to the den, even if the waters waves had reached there already. Only with her strength was Basa able to get the gray one away from the den, but the last puppy of the bunch, a white one, did not want to stay along, grabbing Basa by the fur and dragging her down.

Basa barked and, with her forelegs, pushed the pup away. Nevertheless, the puppy did not give up and went after her. Basa did not care anymore. The pup would perish anyway because Basa had no more strength left in her body. Moreover, when the hard decision came, Basa could only care for those who were chosen to live, and those who were not, had to be left behind to perish. This law Basa could not answer to, and allowed it to lead her every step of the way--- with every step she made.

In the water Basa felt the puppy still clenching to her fur, swimming at her side. When Basa looked back, Basa saw at her side a little round head that would go under and pop up again. The vigorous wild gray pup took all her strength, and Basa became very tired by the time she reached the shore with the gray one. Here, Basa realized, the fourth puppy was not clenching to her fur. Basa ran back to the shore, the dirty waves flapped with reeds and uprooted plants as sedges drifted between some small mammals' dead bodies. Basa could not see the pup anymore. Basa was looking and looking, and a few steps away, some white-looking thing disappeared amidst the dirty water. Basa jumped into the water and with her strong front chest, pushed away the uprooted green carpet of plants and searched for the puppy.

Finally, she touched some slightly moving living creature. Basa grabbed it and took it out to shore. The pup only had a little life left in it, vomiting out all the smelly and dirty water, but very quickly came back to self and happily whimpered in a light tone. The mother took it to the rest of the family and put it on the sedge-and- reeds bedding where they curled up to sleep.

Basa looked at the sleeping, curled up, heavily breathing ball of fur and gave a name to the puppy: Swimmer!

CHAPTER 4

THE UNNAMED
GETTING THEIR NAMES

It was a heavy winter---lots of snow and very cold---when Basa's milk to feed the puppies was becoming less and less. The puppies were very arrogant and, with needle-sharp teeth, made deep marks, wounding their mother's udder. Every feeding was torture for Basa, and her instinct told her that this feeding must be stopped.

The puppies were playing outside in the snow and were waiting for their mother's arrival from the hunt. After merely one step onto the island, Basa was attacked by the puppies. Basa almost lost her footing again. Basa carried them under her udder into the hut, suffering with pain.

The puppies grew a lot in weight and height. The nutrition of Basa's milk was never enough, and the puppies would eat away at their mother's strength. Basa had to get the puppies used to eating the meat. Basa went hunting for two days, watching and stalking the geese that were flying over her head in a big V. Basa finally figured out which block of ice the geese rested on at night. After finding that secret spot, it was easy to find them because their warm bodies made a deep trough into the ice, with a lot of dirt from the birds.

At night Basa watched for opportunity in the nearby reeds. Before daybreak, when the geese were not wide-awake, Basa stealthily went to them until she choked two of the geese. Basa devoured one of them at the kill spot; a little was left over. Basa hid the first goose under the snow. And the other big bird, Basa would take home.

With a clumsy stumble, the puppies came to their mother in the early gray morning. The puppies liked swimming in the deep snow, and with a high pitched yapping voice, they were getting closer to Basa's udder. At front was the gray one and the others followed. At the end, the little one lagged behind, yapping with jealousy. The good and sweet milk of the udder was already in front of them, ready to be grabbed, and in a lightening flash, Basa lashed out at them hard with an angry snarl.

The puppies fell left and right deep in the snow and from there with astonished faces and indignation looked at their mother. What happened to their patient caring mother? Once more the puppies stormed at their mother; but her huge paws swiped them away. Now this game had become serious. The pups were already yapping from pain and disappointment.

Basa put the big goose she had just hunted in front of the puppies and pushed it toward the pups to encourage them to eat. The puppies became quiet and mistrustfully looked at the feathery giant of a goose, who did not move; it only lay down on the snow. Nevertheless, this sight of a dead bird was very frightful to the puppies.

The mother encouraged the puppies to eat once more, and with a commanding and stern growl, pushed the goose gently toward the pups. The little one moved nearer and, with caution and a tail between its legs, went around about it. Finally, the gray one boldly started wildly biting the goose's underbelly and feathers.

One of the goose's legs moved and the pups jumped back. With hair bristled-up and growling with a piping voice, the grey one saw the goose not moving and stealthily got near to it and bit into the feathers of the dead prey. And again, nothing happened in terms of movement so with growling, tearing, ripping, they pulled on the thick feathers.

The feast was unfolding in a bad way. The puppies' noses and mouths were filled with fine feathers. The dogs started sneezing, choking even. The gray pup struggled to vomit and blow all the feathers out by scratching his head with his paws. In the meantime the brothers were trying to tear up the goose; the gray one could not just leave it alone. It did not matter how the small feathers could be that wicked. The gray little wolf started with a new way to attack the goose. Basa watched the puppies for a while, and with a couple of bites, she opened up the goose so the puppies could eat the meat within. The puppies were noisily chewing, growling, and tearing up the goose. The pups licked the fresh blood, snarling at one another out of jealousy. They had eaten meat and tasted blood for the first time, and they liked it.

The pups stood on two hind legs lifting the goose in the air and pushing their heads into the large piece of meat. From there, they yapped and snarled at each other. Only the little runt whined around them. The three bigger pups pushed and squeezed her out of the circle surrounding the goose. Finally, the big three were filled up. They panted with satisfaction and fell down in the snow. Therefore the brothers gave up the meat and allowed the little one get to the goose. The little runt climbed up to the goose's breast and slid into the pot of the meat the brothers had enjoyed and it devoured as much as possible on a kingly table of snow and ice. The mother pulled her, the little runt, out from the bottom of the puppy pile---red from blood. The little one's furry hair already started to turn into frost in the cold winter air.

This was the way the puppies started an independent way of life---when the wild animals became meat eaters instead of milk drinkers. Basa thought it was time to choose a name for them. Basa did not have to wait long. One winter day, Basa was hunting and the puppies were playing by themselves in front of the hut. With delightful excitement they were playing and practicing ways to fight. Two of them clutched each other and rolled over. At that moment, the two others jumped in to make a ruckus after the wild wrestling matches; they separated and sniffed at the fighting grounds.

The puppies exercised; to make their legs and teeth strong and get ready for the upcoming tasks ahead. All of a sudden, the little one became aware that a strange animal was nearing. The animal was white as snow and blended in with the snow. Only the pointy black nose sniffing and a black tuft at the end of his tail gave him away. Sometimes all his four legs were so deep in the snow that it looked like a snake coming toward them with a furry body. The strange animal had short legs but a long body, and his back was moving up and down like a snake when it crept. And in one moment, it disappeared in the snow right in front of their eyes. A couple of yards away, the creature bumped his head out of the snow just like it was coming out of the water.

The creature was shorter than the pups, but with a longer body. First they looked at him with fear in their eyes; especially because his small black eyes were flashing in his sneaky round face. The strange animal slowly crept nearer. The way he was nearing was more funny than fearful.

The puppies, with tilted tails, watched when the little one happily jumped in front of the stranger and called it to play. The strange animal, which was an ermine, jumped on the little ones' back like lightening and the ermines' needle-sharp teeth sank them into the little one's neck. The puppy, like somebody who got struck with terror, shrieked and threw himself up and down to get the deadly rider off of it. The little one fell down into the snow and gave up.

Around her neck was light red blood oozing through her fur. The brothers were frightened from the same terror as the little pup had felt when the ermine attacked her. The brothers hurriedly ran under the hut instinctually for protection. Only in the gray one did the blood of a warrior rise within. Clumsily, but with a fierce temper, the gray pup jumped onto the fast moving weasel, who let go of his victim and now had turned against the gray one. When the little one felt the killer rider let her loose, she yapped with a whimper and ran into the hut.

The gray one was not really a strong opponent against the ermine weasel whose masculine legs were throwing him forward as though he did not even have any body weight.

With his awkward few month old body and the fact that he had not yet lost his milky teeth, his clumsy puppy movements looked very lame against the lightening-fast weasel. Only his tall body and heavy weight could help him in this life-or-death situation. The gray pup was not afraid for a second. A killer instinct brought a red veil over the gray pups' little eyes. On the pups' neck the hair was standing high, and he could see the white attacker. The pups' father, with the savageness of the wolf he was, and Basa's doggish determination came together in him. The gray pup's mother's and father's blood pumped into his heart at once- the two breeds symbolic of his body and character.

The weasel jumped on the gray one's back and sank his teeth into the puppy's neck, looking for the artery. However, right now it was not the little one who was the weasels' opponent. The gray puppy fell back with a rapid movement and tried to rub the weasel off. The weasel, struck again like lightening, and was already on the puppy's belly, between his two front legs, aiming back again at the puppy's throat. The little gray one gave out a loud shriek when the teeth bit into his neck too. Since that occurrence not even a sound was uttered. The weasel and the gray puppy were fighting silently. The weasel jumped left and right, and attacked as the weasels do---always at the neck. The dog tried to put his weight on the quick killer. The snow was flying all over. Deep tracks and craters of footprints showed the marks of the fight. At other times, the weasel would have already let his stubborn prey leave, but lately, he had been unlucky at hunting. The weasels' eyes were burning with hunger, and the gray dog was weakening. The weasel wanted to drink some warm blood, to suck the life out from the gray dog so that he could live on. With a raging madness, the weasel jumped on the foolish puppy dog. The little gray one was at the end of his rope; he would be destroyed and perish. Then, the pup finessed a helpful thought, helping him.

When the weasel jumped at him, the pup quickly lay flat, and when the weasel missed his target and fell next to the gray pup in the snow. The puppy jumped on the white devil; his teeth were closing in on the white neck. The pup now threw his whole body on the snake-like enemy. The dice had rolled and turned the situation around. The weasel threw himself up and down and tried, with his strong nails, to sneak out from under the dog---slicing the dog's belly and shoulder.

The puppy was deeply wounded, blood was all over him. The skin from the pup's head had ripped off halfway by his enemy. Blood constantly flowed into his eyes, turning him half blind. Still, the pup did not let the weasel go; his jaw cramped on the weasel's neck, and nearly unconscious, the pups' whole body lay on the white horror. After a while, the weasel did not move, and his shiny black nose had turned gray. The puppy lay next to him halfway dead, still squeezing the weasel's neck.

They lay like that for a couple moments until the gray one realized that he had won; he was the winner. The white bloodsucker had no life left in him. The pup shook it once more to make sure the weasel was dead; and the weasel's body softly and without resistance swayed in the air. Now, the gray pup let the dead weasel go and stumbled away in the snow rubbing his blinded eyes until he could see again.

Afterward, the gray pup returned to his prey. The other puppies came out from the protection of the hut, and were nearing the pair of fighters cautiously. When they saw the white devil was not moving anymore, they made big jumps and hurried to bask in the glory.

Nevertheless, they found a new enemy in their brother. When they rushed up to bask in the glory, they were met with a brother's jealous growl, attacking and driving them away. And the gray puppy returned to the weasel and started to lacerate the soft body parts, the way he saw his mother do it.

Basa, from far away, felt that something was wrong at home. Unlike the other times when she would travel home so cautiously, she now went home hurriedly through reeds and bushes back to the island, in the deep snow with a young hare in her mouth. The winter birds of the reeds flew away frightened out of Basa's way. As she reached the island, she smelled blood and the terrible smell of the weasel. Rushing up to the kill, she stopped so abruptly that her claws left yards of marks on the frozen surface of the ground.

Two of her puppies stood next to the hut and whimpered jealously at the third gray one who lay above the killed weasel. The gray pup's and the weasel's blood were mixed together as the puppy tore up the white killer's fur. The fourth puppy was not in sight, and amidst the different scents, the pups finally led her to the hut to find the small pup. Basa put down the hare and went to her small puppy, which was still scared to death, and whimpered and tried to reach the wounded throat that she had the idea to lick.

Basa cautiously picked up the puppy and took it out of the hut. Basa examined the fourth pup from nose to tail; she was not hurt seriously, only her neck had many little wounds. Basa helped lick all the blood away and ran to her fourth puppy, still covered in blood.

As the gray pup kept seeing Basa near her puppy, the gray one looked at her and let his head fall onto his prey. Basa wanted to take away the bad-smelling prey, but the puppy went into a rage and attacked his mother, but a few hard slaps brought him back to his senses. Basa finally took the gray wolf pup to the hut to clean off all the blood. The gray one suffered deep wounds, but he did not give out a sound until his mother's stinging tongue licked him all over his wounded body.

The puppy's wolf father came to Basa's memory, and she gave him the name Great Hunter. And for the other wounded puppy, the name Little One would stick with her.

CHAPTER 5

HUNTING SCHOOL

After the trouble with the weasel, Basa used the fox's habit of bringing live prey home, but only the small ones. The dog was not in the habit of teaching their puppies how to hunt because in the world of humans that dogs usually inhabit, there was no need to capture food with strong muscles, teeth, and strong sharp claws. And only with the pin prick of hair-line punctuality could a dog catch prey with such killer instinct experience. The humans usually gave a dog food, that drove a dog for the taste of blood.

Because Basa lived with humans for a long time, she became much smarter, and her ability to adapt was better than the animals of the reeds, and the ancient memory of a hunter broke through her.

The thought came to Basa that it was not enough to just stuff the puppies with food. Basa needed to teach them the easiest way to get meat out of necessity. Basa went back to the ancient time of raising puppies in concordance to the way of life they now had, human-free.

When observing the ordinary dog, puppies did not usually hunt, only when they were already grown-ups, and even that was just for fun. However, Basa's puppies would be dead from starvation because the reeds laws were relentless. If you wanted to eat, you needed to be faster, stronger, and cleverer than your prey. And if you were weak, you would die because here in the reeds, there was no human household waiting to take care of you and give you a piece of food all the time.

For the first time, Basa brought home a live black-and-white duck to the dogs' hut. The puppies were looking at the duck sheepishly, and with suspicion. Even Great Hunter walked around the feathered stranger in a cautious way. The duck, with blinking eyes, was frightened to death in Basa's mouth. Basa put the duck in front of the pups with an encouraging growl, but none of the puppies had the courage to get at the prey.

The duck, with horror, panted between the giant four-legged animal---Basa. Then Basa realized in her little mind, that the duck's wings were free. Basa stood up and, after a couple of steps ---the meat was already in the air. If Basa was unable to catch the duck in flight, there would be no lunch for her today. The puppies started dancing excitedly when they saw the prey flying away. Basa became smart; with one bite she broke the duck's wing and put it down. Basa moved aside, for she was not afraid. The duck was a really bad runner, was not able to escape. The puppies, craving meat out of hunger, were alarmed and jumped around the little black bird who was sitting like a black sod without feeling on the white snow. But even Basa's encouraging growl did not help the puppies. Their bravery was only enough for a start and quick-stopping break. If the duck would have tried to run away, they would probably jump on it because they would just be playing, different than attacking prey. However, sitting as it was, the black duck looked like a frightened stranger.

Now, Basa forced the duck to move with her nose, and the duck, feeling it would still be able to escape, stood up and tried her broken wings. But that did not work, so she clumsily shuffled to shore. The puppies started shrieking when they saw the food leaving; what would be of their lunch?

When the duck started to move, Great Hunter flattened his earflap, stiffened his legs, and with big jumps got on to catch the escapee. Great Hunter grabbed the duck, squeezed it, and tore into it. It took time to kill the bird. After sitting on his prey with a wild growl, he ran off to the other newly-brave puppies.

Basa needed to teach a lesson to her selfish gray puppy so the others would be able to get some meat. But the others were still afraid of their brother. All three of them went to the other side of the duck and left the Great Hunter alone. Even after that, the gray one was still offensive toward the other pups with his righteousness. The gray pups shrieking signaled that he was not only going to eat the duck, but was also going to be a tyrant to the weaker family members.

The next day, a bun duck was the prey again. The puppies were not afraid of this one, not as much as from the first one from the day before. The pups finished the duck together. Even the Little One acted bravely. The next big step was coming ahead; gathering the knowledge and the courage to finish the prey alone, one by one.

Basa did not break the duck's wings this time as she had before. Basa let her puppies learn how to catch a clumsy laboring, flying duck, halfway on the ground; halfway in the air. Swimmer started approaching first. Basa put the duck down. Swimmer was nearing without hesitation and waited. The duck started with and awkward movement and flew upward. Finally, Swimmer jumped up but his jaws missed the target. With a silly face, Swimmer looked after the flying long-necked prey.

Basa did not care and let the pups become hungry. The pups learned through the hunger in their bellies how to pay for being clumsy and unskillful. Nevertheless, the duck would not be so easy to catch all the time. Basa felt as though this summertime prey of a duck would be the easiest to teach the puppies. However, this time of year in winter, the field vole and the meadow mouse were hiding and sleeping. The small birds were very rare. There truly was not much selection out there. Basa caught whatever she could catch. An old gander goose with a big hard beak was now the rival opponent. Basa beckoned Great Hunter to be the first to attack without hesitation, but the gander goose had such a strong beak that it knocked him on the head and stretched Great Hunter out on the snow.

Swimmer was next, and was not lucky either. Swimmer's nose was sliced up by the goose's hard beak. And "no name yet" got beat into the snow with two flashes of the wings. The Little One was the only one with a brain who did not attack the strong gander. Aside from sneaking around with a waving tail, snatching into the thick goose feathers- The Little One did not accomplish much---almost as though she was only poking him with a reed stick. Finally, Basa finished the aggressive gander, and the shameful puppies barely touched the meat.

Still, the prey at paw was mostly wild duck. Basa needed to go to the large section of the reeds to get one out of the loud flock. Now, Great Hunter was on the line again to show his knowledge. The Great Hunter still remembered his failure with the last goose. The duck was flying up.

Great Hunter jumped and at once fell on the snow, growling with triumph. After a while, all four of the pups were able to catch the flying feathered- game, even the Little One.

The "no name yet" became an especially skillful, capable hunter. "No name yet" was very agile and quicker than his family members. When "No name yet" jumped, it was like he was flying in the air after the escaping prey, and he sometimes caught the prey so high in the air that even Basa was surprised by it. The Great Hunter did not let his prey move when he caught it. The other two pups would catch prey any way they could, but "no name yet" teased his prey, giving the prey possibilities for escape.

After a lot of feathered game at the end of the winter, Basa brought home one already-shedding, thick-furred hare. Basa made sure the hare would not run away easily by breaking one of its hind legs, but even with that reinforcement, the hare would be able to run faster than the puppies if it was trying to escape. The hair was a never-seen-before animal. The puppies gazed at it with big open eyes.

Great Hunter, who was only interested in the end-result, wanted to kill the hare he held down right away. Basa did not let him. Besides, Basa set free the hare in front of the pups, and the hare ran away very fast on his three legs.

The puppies, with great enthusiasm, eagerly ran after the fast-running prey. The pups ran shoulder to shoulder except for the quick,"No Name Yet" who flew with his long legs at top speed ahead of the yapping puppies and left them behind in the distance. The puppies started crying in unison, a chorus of a hunters notes. But, the chorus was not going to stop the escaping hare, which disappeared from the island, and cut into the reeds. The puppies chase ended at the shore of the island. The pups stopped and, with disappointment, headed back home.

The hare was a very interesting, exciting animal to have encountered; unlike the smelly stupid feathered birds and ducks. Now, the hare was running away like lightening. But, one of the puppies, "No name yet", was still pursuing the hare. Basa made a growl after him to stop, but with wide jumps, he disappeared into the reeds. Whatever you could still see at the top of the moving reeds was where the hunting went on. At once, everything became quiet. After a long while, the puppy came out from the reeds and carried a lifeless hare in his jaw. This occurrence is how he got his name, and ever since they called him "Runner".

Until the snow thawed away, Basa brought the food and prey home. However, when the first migrating bird shrieks were heard in the beautiful spring sky, Basa let the puppies test their own strength. The puppies had gotten everything from their mother that a mother could give. The puppies' play-time was over. At six months old, their milk teeth became iron-hard fangs.

The puppies learned how to kill a prey. For the rest of the pups much needed pursuit of knowledge---how to find and capture the prey on their own---the reeds would inevitably teach them these lessons.

CHAPTER 6

HUNTERS

Swimmer, one big-sized dog was stealthily nearing the shore of the water. Between the thick reeds, Swimmer crawled and hid, and it looked like he did not care how dirty his white furry coat became from the dirty, swampy, water. On the open water, all kinds of water-birds swam naively without guile. The big white dog, Swimmer, stalked and crawled after them like a cat. Sometimes, Swimmer stood up listening. At that time, you would be able to see that his head and legs were not proportionate, which were still a sign of his puppy age.

In body and size, Swimmer was above average compared to most dogs. Swimmer was a big white dog, and he owned the water shore; that was his kingdom. The birds and their smell were protected by the big open water as they conceitedly paraded. It was almost impossible to get near them, especially on the open water, but actually going into the water would help. The risky circumstance of the open water is what incited Swimmers' instincts to excite. Suddenly, Swimmer lay flat. A reed moved, and a small reed warbler blinked in front of Swimmer, paying attention to the dog with cunning. So the little big-mouthed spy of a warbler did not give up its whereabouts. However, the little cackling bird was not easy to fool. The bird turned its head sideways with a turn, it was looking-looking, and started the warning call;

tiri, tiri, tara, chit, chet, tir, tir. The birds' little throat was shaking proudly as it looked down while sounding the warning call. The warbler would not let the hiding puppy dog out of sight. Swimmer, made himself seem seemingly dead. Still, the reeds' private eye did not stop the alarm.

The Little One would have stumbled away in shambles, a long time ago. Runner would probably stop the busy little feathered bugger with a lightening jump. Swimmer on the other hand was a stubborn dog. Although Swimmer was persistent he was a little simple-minded and patiently hid between the sharp reeds, hoping the warbler would get bored and stop. Nevertheless, the warblers' throat was not getting tired, and with blinking eyes, he found the dog and started pecking and chirping away at him.

It seemed like the bird wanted to torture Swimmer. Sometimes, even a peaceful bird or animal had an instinctive self-defense mechanism, and had a longing aggressive desire to torture the foe that came rushing at them; breaking the idealistic life of the colony. Not many animals were able to stand the uproar--- the hubbub--- that birds like these could make. Swimmer was shaking from anger: he could do nothing against his torturer. The little, feathered, field guard was alert. Nothing could betray or bribe his watchful eyes away.

Finally, the dog lost his patience. It did not matter how stubborn Swimmer could be. The water-birds listened to the warbler's alarm and moved away, swimming far into the open water. Swimmer stretched out his stiff, numb, legs and did not care about the loudmouth bird anymore. Swimmer went anywhere that he could not hear the warbler's wicked sound.

What Swimmer would really have liked to do was to hide in some big hole, but Swimmer was too big to fit in any badger-made hole. The only choice he had was to go after the bird, but the warbler was more stubborn than Swimmer. She was probably protecting her nest.

Mocking him, shrieking at him, jumping above him from reed to reed; wherever he went, she sometimes stayed back a little while, and when Swimmer thought he was free from the noise, the warbler dangled above him on the reed in the next moment; tri, tri, chet, chet,-

-- blaring into his ear. Swimmer's eyes became red with anger, and he let out a deep growling sound at the bird. This had no effect; it looked like this was going to ruin the day for hunting. Still, the warbler did not stop, jumping above the dogs' head, coming down to the reed leaves, attacking the back of her victim; because of these actions, even Swimmer's peaceful mood could not bear it any longer, and with a sudden leap into the air, the conceited chit-chatterer barely escaped from the dog's clapping jaws.

The horrified bird shrieked and stopped, falling into the reeds. Swimmer was happy with the result; he was able to get rid of his tormentor. At once, Swimmer became stiff. Swimmer was lifting one leg up, and his tail was nervously shaking. From far away, Swimmer heard some barking. Runner was chasing some kind of game. Swimmer recognized the sound of Runner's voice. Swimmer ran through everything in his way to find the hunting ground where his agile brother was hunting. Alone, Swimmer's hunting day was already lost.

Since morning time, Runner had been sniffing and looking for game. And so, in front of his nose was a big gray hare leaping high in the air and out of the reeds; what a big boy it was! Runner became scared at first, for he did not know from where the big rumbling noise was coming from. When he saw the big hare running away, he became agitated; and with a loud bark, ran after the escaping hare. The hare was an old boy, a very cunning and artful player of the hunting game; a couple of times, he would look back and make fun of Runner who was trying so hard. So many dogs and wolves had chased him before--- all of them had to run after the hare until their lungs exploded. With a few fast loops, the hare made a fool of them, and the hunter stopped without knowing how to go ahead and continue. The hare was running comfortably without looking back; he could hear the dog chasing behind him. With his long ears, folding behind his head, it looked as though his body was twice as long. The hare looked like he was flying above the earth.

The cracking of the reeds and hissing of the leaves were still at the old boy's heels, who was scared now. Even though other dogs and wolves had chased this hare before, never had he had an encounter with a quick-legged pursuer like Runner. The hare tried to trick the dog; he leapt high, jumped right, made a roundabout, and disappeared into the reeds. Runner had a hard time stopping his stride when the hare dealt this trick. Runner was sliding on his two hind legs, almost toppled over, and by the time he turned around---his would-be prey had disappeared. Runner put his nose on the ground to trail the scent, but it took some time until he figured out the roundabout way. With a happy bark, he jumped into the reeds and held his nose close to the scent in order to pursue the prey, the hare that had escaped.

The trick master was running comfortably again. The hare felt it was safe already. At one side of the hare was the wide water, and at the other side were thick tall reeds. It would be easy for the hare to escape whenever he wanted. The hare even stopped to sit and listen at one point. That was how sure the hare was of himself. One of his ears looped and dangled downward, he looked around. The hare was sitting quietly, and Runner was still far away; the hare knew that Runner was far away because of how the reeds were moving around him. Nevertheless, for the faint-hearted hare, the moving reeds were enough of a signal to keep up the running; going through an opening, where the hare got out of the reeds a different white dog---Swimmer--- rushed at him. Struck with horror as all the prey were during the possibility of their capture, the hare jumped to the side and into the water.

Swimmer chased the hare, barking with the heat of the hunt, pursuing and running after the hare. One swimming after the other, a little round brown head with big long ears and a big white face, realized Swimmer was nearing, Runner heard Swimmer barking and ran toward the sound of the barking. From the opening, Runner jumped into the water. Although Runner was a good swimmer too, he did not like soaking his fur. However, with dogs of the reeds, these dogs needed to do many things that they probably did not like. By this time, for the hare, the situation became too hot. The hare climbed to shore and fled in a hurry. Swimmer and Runner were after him.

The two dogs were running straight then broke around the reeds, and the birds flew away. Both the pursuers and the pursued strength were nearing an end. The hare looked back more often, and he made more and more roundabouts.

The hare would have been able to outrun the quick and agile Runner had Runner been by himself; for he was still just a puppy. However, outnumbered, the two dogs were able to overtake him. One dog was pursuing and the other dog would cut the hare off. Runner and Swimmer were pressing from both sides of the leaping prey. Runner almost caught the hare from behind once. Runner was already barking with victory when the long-eared hare with a giant leap jumped into the air. The dogs tipped over. The hare fell down on Runner's back, jumped away and ran away again.

Underneath one thick bush, Great Hunter was deep asleep. When Great Hunter heard the hunters' ruckus, Great Hunter sat up, still dazed from sleep and blinked for a few moments. Great Hunter recognized Runner's high-pitched sound and Swimmer's deep bark. From the sound of their voices, Great Hunter figured out that his brothers were pursuing a field hare. Great Hunter wondered whether or not he should join Runner and Swimmer. Aside from Runner, Great Hunter was a better runner than all of the other puppies. Right now, Great Hunter was lazy and sluggish from his sleep and was not in the mood for a long run and possibly unsuccessful hunt. Great Hunter was listening with his head raised up. With a quick decision, Great Hunter crossed through roads and track-marks, hurrying to the edge of the reeds.

To catch prey, Great Hunter never thought about the prey as some unseen power. Moving his strong body into the best position, Great Hunter was sure that the hare would come out from the reeds where he was taking guard, just before the open field started. The old boy, the cunning hare, ran to the edge of the reeds; the hares' eyes were popping out of its sockets. In the open fields, the hare could run with more ease, tiring Runner and Swimmer---the stubborn dogs. The lights came through the end of the reeds, and there was less water the hare had to muddle through. From the last willow tree, everything was open to the free, waving field of grass. The hares' instincts made him much faster while running past the willow tree.

At that moment, from behind the bush, a giant gray animal jumped straight for the hare's neck. Great Hunter, the grey animal, only had time for one strike. Great Hunter broke the hare's back, and sat with satisfaction over his prey. Runner and Swimmer, with loud barking, urged forward from the reeds, and in front of them Grey Hunter sat over the hare with malicious joy. With their tongues hanging out, Runner and Swimmer came toward Grey Hunter with happy faces. Great Hunter, with a growl of an enemy's expression, made a signal that the prey belonged to him alone. The hare was not for sharing, not even a piece of hair.

With a surprised and astonished look from the two other brothers, the Great Hunter, who with a ruler's dominion, turned his back on Runner and Swimmer; opened the hare up. Great Hunter got used to the fact that the others were afraid of him; he already beat them one by one when they revolted against his rule. In addition, after a bitter experience, not one of them challenged his superiority. Swimmer and Runner just looked at him, imploringly and hungrily, until Great Hunter opened up the soft part of the hare's body. From the smell of the blood, Swimmer and Runner angrily attacked the despot. In addition, a huge great fight started. The two white-haired dogs beat up Great Hunter.

The gray Great Hunter was forced to comply. Now all three of the brothers lacerated the hare and growled at each other angrily if they saw one of them tearing a bigger piece of meat than the other. The Little One did not yet know how to come around and get its prey. Great Hunter, with a kingly gesture, gave the hares' head to The Little One. The Little One chewed on the prey until Basa came around, and out of mercy gave The Little One a piece of her own prey. Basa's litter became the rulers of the reeds.

CHAPTER 7

LITTLE ONE

It was not by chance that her name was Little One. Little One was the weakest of the litter. They could have named her The Last One because she was born last and got the last nipple; she was also the last one who could eat when her mother, Basa, brought the prey home. Little One was destined for now to get the wings, feet, and head. From those parts only some juicy marrow and the brains was good enough, but not enough to build muscles and strong bones. The accident with the weasel left a mark on her: in the wound-fever, she did not grow or get strong. However, Little One became smarter and more sensitive than the others.

If we wanted to characterize Little One on a human scale, you could say that she had become a nervous dog. Next to her giant brothers, Little One resembled a medium-sized dog. Surprisingly, Little Ones' bark was frightful; she had a deep hoarse-sounding bark that did not fit her appearance---or her tame and cunning look. If we are talking about Little One, we need to say honestly that we like to show our heroes in the best character and form they have. The only thing we cannot say about Little One is that she was brave.

However the writer found an excuse and found the leniency for what the hero---Little One---lacked. Little One's nervous sensitivity and smarts were not a good ground for her bravery to plant roots and grow, as the same way it would not for a human. Since the incident with the weasel from when Little One was a puppy, The Little One's days of sickness was decisive on the way her character would be formed. Little One was playful with adulation, but at times, she was inclined towards private quietness and sadness in the dark abandoned shepherd hut. When the cold, hard winter came, it sucked out the little energy Little One still had. By the time the spring warmed the waters under its sunshine---Little One---would stagger from one place to another with weak legs and nothing but skin and bone. Little One did not take part in her brothers' hunting for a long time.

Little One ate what Basa gave Little One out of her motherly love, or what Great Hunter gave Little One out of generosity. Little One roamed the reeds and watched the birds' migration and their hunting, how they made their nests. Very soon, she became more knowledgeable of mysteries behind the great grassy meadows than Basa was. Little One was able to sit under the red warblers' nest for long hours. Little One was hoping the soft young birds would fall out of their nest so Little One could have her own prey. Most of the time, Little One's expectations became disappointments because all the little birds ever did was open their big hungry mouths for food. None of the birds were in the mood to fall out. The Little One soon realized that hunting the way she was hunting was comfortable, but not useful. After the realization about the birds, the fish caught her attention but sooner or later, Little One saw that not one of the fish wanted to come out to the shore.

Moreover, in the water, the fish were extremely lively. Little One kept going over to where the edge of the reeds were, where the grassy field became wet. Little One was willing to wait at certain dry places, watching a mouse hole for hours just to get a couple of soft mouthfuls of meat. On the other hand, Little One waited for a porcupine that Little One turned over onto its backside. The porcupine, out of curiosity, poked his nose out from his thorny protection---that was when the Little One put her paw on the belly of the porcupine. The price for that was a couple of thorns in her nose to get the soft, tender meat.

One day, a falcon hit a duck in the air and the duck fell down onto the grasslands. Little One chased away the shrieking falcon and ate the duck by herself. From that day on, Little One never missed out on a possibility of looking up the sky and hoping for a present. Little One's weaker development made her more observant than her wild and aggressive brothers. Little One got prey all the time. Little One's experience in observing prey led her on the right track. Little One was looking for the easiest prey all the time, and that type of hunt she was not able to give up---even when the time came when she was already becoming strong and would be able to catch any wild game in the reeds. No matter how much Little One ate; she still never shied away from asking her strong brothers for some extra food.

If Little One needed it, she could steal away the best piece of meat of either Swimmer's or Runner's share. However, when the two brothers realized the missing food, Little one was already walking around with the face of a thousand angels, and if worse came to worse, Little One would bravely take a beating for having stolen the food.

To find an answer for Little One's behavior, Little One's eating habits probably came from when she was a puppy. Little One could not forget her hunger, and by the time she had already grown up, she could eat until she got sick and it was still not enough. Apart from the human being, no other animal could be indulged with such ravenous hunger as Little One. The Little One became spoiled because the food she once greatly missed and now was getting filled her up as though she was being pampered. From springtime to fall, there was an unfailing "open table" in that habitat. Little One found her open-food table in the springtime to be a present from the reeds.

Little One found the real secret of the island, what not even the oldest fishermen were able to discover---an island of birds. The big meadow eagle was her guide. When Little One saw the big eagle push down from the air one common heron, and as the Little One heard the eagles' sharp and loud cry over the dead prey, Little One tried to get closer to the eagle. Above Little One, in the sky like a dark cloud, all kinds of birds zigzagged and that made Little One's mind more curious. Carefully, Little One jumped from one marshy bog to the other and neared the spot where the big eagle landed.

The regular way of the reeds, was to follow the islands and patches of dry land. The space in between marshy bog to marshy bog was as wide as two-hundred feet, and you could not see a single reed. And between the marshy bogs, there was smelly, deadly thick black water, and in a rotting bull-rush, there were swimming beetles and leeches. Little One would not know that those green head tops of the bogs were two- yard-long swaying plants sitting on top of a tower of loose soil. And if you fell off from the marshy bog into the water, you would never be able to get out of the black water.

The leeches would suck you dry, and the swimming beetle would chew you until the white bones went under and into the deep mud. However, Little One's instinct whispered the danger into her ear, and she was crouching with a terrified feeling at the first swaying marshy bog. In front of her, the swamp had a narrow promenade that was covered with thin sparse reeds, and further above, there was a pearly shine to the open water and clouds of birds.

Little One could not stay away from the rich sight of lots of food and, with a stumbling movement, began to go on to the marshy bog. The next marshy bog moved under Little One, and she almost fell into the water. With a quick rapid jump, Little One reached the third marshy bog that lie there. The third marshy bog Little One jumped on still moved under her. Little One's heart was beating and she was jumping very fast from one bog to another; this described Little One's luck. If Little One moved slowly she could never make it alive out of the black water.

That was how all the shepherd dogs learned---like science---for long periods of time one would only be able to go on the marshy bog if one ran, otherwise one would fall into the water. Out of fear, Little One learned within a minute that she was in danger. Finally, Little One was shaking and trembling on the last piece of land she had jumped on. Shining like ice in front of her was the flat water, but she was already safe. Further up on the glassy water were the shrieking birds of the island. The eagle was ready to move on. Flapping with a few clumsy strokes of its wings, and a gangly run, the eagle slowly lifted its heavy body and disappeared into the sky. Little One was not sorry for the big eagle's departure.

Little One would not like to pick a quarrel with a strong looking bird. On the other side of the island, the big shining open water lost its glitter, overrun by sedge and bulrush and other plants. Roots and decayed and crumbling planks of wood, with twine coiled around it, made a thick carpet atop the water. Hair and dead fish with silver colors gave a design on the green surface. The sweet smell of the rotten plants and the stench of decayed fish settled in the air. At the end of the open water sat a decaying small island, breaking away with willow trees and bushes. The way the island was situated, like a ship with a willow tree as its sail---like a crowned jewel--- the birds were nesting on the twigs and bushes. Since there were few big trees, and those trees that were big had been stripped of their wood, the birds on the island sat above what was underneath the short trees---fish parts! The birds!

Little One's head became dizzy from all of the noise and movement. All of the water with the whole reeds, trees, and even the sky looked like it was flying, shrieking, turning. Everywhere on the waters, in the air, and on the trees---the birds were uncountable. It was nesting time. All over the island, it was filled with birds who sat on eggs. At the edge of the water, huge nests of battonyos were gathered tightly together on the reed sticks. The egret nest was out of reach. In the clear water, shadows of big fishes glided away in front of Little One's legs. The pike was looking for prey, and without even a little movement, only the lightly moving gill gave away the hungry grabber. The ongoing noise, smells, warming and milling of the water, made Little One mad. Little One jumped into the water and swam on to the big island.

Little One found herself in the middle of a war because the army of birds frightened her, and alarming shrieks and wings flapping beat Little One back into the water. On Little One's third try, she got brave enough and climbed onto shore, where the birds were still bothering her, but she felt more secure when she realized the fast flying white birds would not hurt her. Before they could hit her, with a quick turn at the last second they flew away like an arrow shooting nearby Little One's head. Little One shook herself, and after that, Little One did not care about the birds anymore. In front of the birds' nests, there were thousands of egg-breeding birds. Little One felt that it all belonged to her as a reward for her courage and clever wide-awake moves. What got her into that situation? The Little One was hungry. And Little One started with the abandoned eggs of a sitting brooding mother that had left the nest with a terrifying shriek. At the edge of the nests were little yellow cracked egg shells, marks of Little One's appetite and clumsiness.

First, Little One ate through the presents the nests bestowed onto her. After that Little One started picking of her choice. Little One liked the red-headed duck and the green-with--touch- of- grey eggs. Little One liked colored eggs. Nevertheless Little One left with disgust. The battonya's soft thick eggs were covered with dirt. The fathers of the eggs flew around Little One's head with anger, but she sometimes barked at them and because of that she seemed courageous. And besides, no enemy was around that Little One should be afraid of. When Little One's belly became full and she could not eat anymore eggs, she drank one and lay down under a bush. The mother birds were still flying around, and after a while, they dared to come down and check on their nests right by Little One. From that day on, Little One was never too lazy to make a trip onto the birds' island. But Little One was very prudent about it; Little One would be the last one who climbed out of the hut by the time all of her brothers left to hunt. Little One was afraid if the others discovered her loot, she would be left behind with only leftovers.

One day, Runner became aware that Little One's mouth was covered with yellow egg yolk. Runner grabbed Little One by the neck and shook her, just as he would do to the rats. Runner shook her so that Little One would show him where to find the eggs. Little One was whimpering and struggling, but bravely took the torture until Great Hunter---who held the Little One as one of his own court jesters---took her away from Runner's punishing jaw with his own powerful bites. But that time, Runner, who was receiving a blow at that time, was too late because many of the eggs had hatched. The eggs hatching became an even better scenario than before because many little birds, for a long time, were much clumsier in the water than Little One was. And the meats! For a long time, Little One could not forget the little fluffy birds. There were so many birds milling on the island that a dirty, hungry dog like Little One could take a tax on them and still, you would not miss one. There would presently be a lot more birds milling around. Moreover, because of the one mouth of Little One, the little fluffy birds did not seem like they were missing. During that time, Little One became fat and heavy, and her stomach rounder in comparison to any other wild dog. Little One looked unfit and had a shameful appearance.

The other present the island left for Little One were the three big trees where the big black fisher birds were nesting, and they were masters of fishing. Under the trees there was a huge amount of bird dirt, waste, and food remnants that the young birds did throw down: Little One unwillingly went over there because she was considered a clean dog as far as a wild dog can be a clean dog. With time, the young birds became less catchable. The birds became too fast and quick in the water for Little One. So she had to check out the trees, and with her luck, maybe one of the young fisher birds would fall off their nest.

The old birds became agitated as Little One neared the trees. The young birds did not fall down for Little One, but with a deafening shriek threw all the fish that were in the nests on the back of Little Ones' head. With a loud thump, all the big fishes came down, like carps and bleaks. After a couple of hits, she had to jump sometimes to avoid getting hurt. After a short time, when Little One became aware of all the fish shortage in the water, she picked the biggest pieces of fish the birds threw to her to eat--- she was even able to hide some of it. Since then, the fisher birds hunted for Little One too. Little One only needed to go under the trees, bark a couple times, and fat fishes came down like missiles. And the day came when Little One stumbled through the marshy bogs in vain with no fish, no eggs, and all the newborns winged away. Little One was sitting on the shore for a long time with a hungry stomach as she looked up to the sky where all the birds were flying and zigzagging away. After a while, Little One went home, and by evening, she was again getting a share of Basa's and Great's prey.

CHAPTER 8

Where the reeds ended and the grass meadow began, a young fox wandered lazily in the thick and high grass, sniffing and looking around. One could see by the young fox's body language that it was not in the grass hunting for food but was only playing in the field. However, if some light prey came up to it like a newborn hare or a small mouse, it would be a nice catch. At this time of the year, a good hunter had to watch out for every detail because the reeds were filled with little animals like the hare: the hares give birth every six weeks, but if you were lucky, you could catch the mother full of unborn babies. The mother hare would be slower at this time. And a young fox thought of himself as a good hunter. All the way through the fox's journey in the meadow he was sniffing and traversing across the land with a hind leg scratching the flea attack he got from his dirty and smelly foxhole.

The fox found a cold hare den by surprise and gave out a tiny bark that was not exactly suitable for a hunter's profile. For a few steps, the fox followed the hare's cold scent and stopped and started to scratch himself again. Little One was watching the fox from the edge of the reeds. Little Ones' nose was being bothered by the sharp leaves of the reeds, but she would not move away; she herself had a lot of desire to learn. Little One had never met a fox before and did not know how strong it was and what kinds of behaviors it had. The smell of the fox brought out Little Ones' dislikes; she found the red fox's behavior provocative. Little One saw the fox was a meat eater and that it could be a dangerous animal. The fox quickly froze up.

The fox's long bushy tail straightened out. Only the white tassel at the end of his tail shook when lifting up its two front legs. Little One watched with agitation at what the fox was going to catch. On the account of Little One, the fox's red fur was now right in front of her nose. The fox jumped, and Little One's sharp eyes could see through the grass that a fat mouse was now in the fox's mouth. The red fur was ahead of Little One, catching the light of the sun. The fox's red hair was like glowing embers, shining like a sharp light, even if it was still wearing its old shabby summer coat. Little One was bothered by the thought that the fox caught a mouse that she believed to be her own.

Little One should punish the fox for its audacity, but it looked like a tough and agile animal. Little One was much bigger, but even the smallest of animals could beat the biggest. Little One did not forget the ermine from her youth, and she thought it was better for the fox to await its punishment.

The white dog stepped out of the bush. The fox was against the wind and did not see the dog. Then all of a sudden, it turned around like a cowboy's whip and gave a big hiss to the big white dog. As she pushed forward out from the reeds and ran with a long stretched body into the dense plant life, Little One made a brave jump, going after the fox. Now she was ready to give punishment for the fox's transgression with the mouse. Little One pursued the fox until the reeds began, and with a calm satisfaction, went back into the grass sniffing out the cold hare den she had found before. Even she felt the smell of a mouse, but no meat. Little One was hungry; she went around into the meadow's grass. Behind the grass, it seemed that the endless marshy midday calmness was only there, and in the air of a blue, blue, sky the thick green reeds along with a few trees stood out.

On the meadow grass, you could see some willows, small brooks, a few reeds with water lily, orange flames, and other small yellow-white flowers at the wet bottoms. The grass was covered with a gray dry mud from where the spring flood drew up. Farther on, where the flood did not reach were thick and green blades of grass. The tree trunks showed the gray waterline. In the idyllic atmosphere, the bees buzzed on flowers and sleepy green flies flickered. The big blue dragonfly hunted for mosquitoes that were flying back and forth.

In front of Little One was a small brown grasshopper jumping up and down. Not one of the large animals moved. Only the grass swished sometimes, and from time to time, a reed rustled. The only thing you were able to see was a white dog, but she too lay motionless. As a human, you could fall under the spell of the idyllic peace and quiet. From a hunter's point of view, Little One thought all this was natural. Playfully, she tried to catch grasshoppers, but even that did not break the spell of peace and quiet. Little One looked back to the reeds. Her tongue covered her bottom teeth and lightly shook as protection from the heat.

Little One checked on the sky. Who knows? Hopefully, some big eagle or other bird of prey could be circling around, but it was better not to pick on them. Between the flat and faraway trees, were some white flashes showing a human house. Little One did not know what that was because she had never seen a human. Basa mostly did not go out of the reeds. They never really went out deep into the grass meadow together. To go there was a very strong prohibition, a beating and biting prohibition. Basa's puppies were missing the easiness of being in a human household, and on top of that they were missing the fox's instinct of impudent risk-taking. However, Little One understood the prohibitions that lay before her and did not interfere with them. She believed only in her own experience: she felt disdain even for her brothers. She thought; Swimmer and Runner are stupid and Great Hunter was bloodthirsty and crazy. For the puppies, the prohibition of the house was the end of the line they would not step over. And Little One, the coward, was not afraid until the powerful mystery of the prohibition presented itself due to many bites of experience. She succeeded in finding a hare's scent. It was an old scent that Little One still followed.

Little One was so much an inhabitant of the reeds that she did not show herself while hunting, as the domesticated dogs that lived amongst humans, would do. Through the hills of grass, from one bush to another; by way of precaution, she tested her knowledge. Moreover she would rather like to run because she was happy. As far as Little One could see, her own feet were the firm, solid earth. The run almost called to her, it was not like the reeds where there was the constant danger of life and surprise threats. She drank from the crystal clear brook and watched the water bug quickly hiding under the stones. The water was so clear the fly's body made a shadow at the bottom of it.

A motionless, gray, egret stood almost imperceptibly in the distance. On the way towards it, Little One went farther, to where the water grass became less green, the brook had dried up, and the dirt was much drier. Slowly she arrived to the land that belonged to the humans; she arrived to the wheat fields where at the edge she found a narrow tread down road. A long time ago, Little One left the hares' scent on the small road, and she found many more but at this point did not care for it anymore. It would be hopeless to chase a hare during midday while it was resting in its den, and even the trail was not leading all the way to where the hare was resting. With a few great jumps, the hare would lose the trail's scent. And even if Little One found one, she would not be able to catch it.

Little One went into the wheat field; however, she was uncomfortable to walk in. As it seems, cut out at the other side of the field, the fate of where Little One was situated held a lot of experience for her. She almost ran into a white tomcat. Never having seen a cat before, she only smelled a wildcat's scent sometime in the reeds, which was a very rare animal. Both of them became frightened. Little One trembled from anger because the tomcat's irritating smell ate into her bones.

And, Little One, the coward and light-hearted, who thought about and considered everything, with a dark cast over her eyes, attacked the cat. From left to right, the cat slapped Little One with sharp claws. Little One started bleeding on both sides under her eyes, and the cats' claws got into her bones. She felt a great pain, and through her closed eyes, felt many small pinpricking, side- splitting pains. At once, Little One's premeditated, clever, self-control came to her. If you were to think of it we could praise Little One for having her frame of mind return to her, because it came back with a common sense; a common sense that could make a human wonder. This is how heroes were born. In the animal kingdom, except for a few examples, animals would rather relate to a state of madness.

From a few steps away, Little One was watching the cat. He was still hissing and blowing with an arched back, and he would not take his yellow-green eyes off Little One. The tomcat's claws were sliding in and out. Little One could not calm down completely; she would like to break that bendable white spine back, but those claws! The claws! Carefully with instinct, Little One tried to reach and lick her wounded face with her tongue. She could not reach it. And the wound was itching and throbbing. Little One needed a new type of warfare, and delivered with an old dog behavior; she started barking with a deep throat and rugged sound. Once in a while, Little One raised her voice to the highest pitch. If Great Hunter were there, he definitely would tear into her because he got disgusted by unnecessary noise during the hunt. Luckily, the gray brother was faraway prowling the reeds.

So Little One could bravely sing her tune. She danced around the cat and made fake attacks, making sure her body did not get too close to those dangerous claws. Little One's feet were planted into the ground with her own claws, making deep marks on the dry road. The cat always turned herself face to face after the dancing dog. The tomcat was an old warrior. He had already handled a bigger threat than this one in his life. So when Little One pulled back and enjoyed her own voice, the cat turned around and ran away. And the dog ran after the cat. Actually Little One was happy that she did not have to fight with the round headed predator. She was not about to catch the escaping cat who was running with a stretched-out body.

However, the hunting fever caught fire and the rushing blood in Little One's veins added to the excitement of her pursuit. And Little One, with her menacing bark, ran after the cat. She stopped so abruptly and almost fell over her head. She had lost the cats' scent. Somewhere, he cut to the other side into the high growing grass where Little One could not see him from the wheat field's jagged and uneven corners. Little One turned around with her nose to the ground. She found a cold hare's and bird's scent, but she could not find the sickening hateful scent of the tom-cat. Little One's sense of smell was so delicate, like the finest spider-web that could catch all the unseen, flying, world of scent. At the sight of a bunch of blue cornflowers, a big blowfly got stuck, and Little One got the lost scent of the cat back from there. The sense in her whispered to better leave the tomcat alone. She had done enough for showing her bravery requirements, and she did consider it as a shame to herself to abandon the trail. However some hidden commander that Little One never before had found in herself---telling her, go get him. No one knew who that commander could be. It could have been the instinct that was commanding the nervous system, a passion for hunting that was one branch of the instinct, or it could be a vanity (the dog could have a vanity). The vanity belonged to her common sense and that was not a small branch anymore.

Little One was not rebellious in nature. The command could come from anyone. She would not refuse openly, but avoid it; she was a master of evasion. The unseen commander lived in herself---in her teeth, veins, and muscles. Little One could not just shamble away. She was not so much in the mood; however, she was still in the heat of excitement. Little One picked up the scent and went after the tomcat again. Probably never in her life had she jumped that high a fence when she stepped over that small clod of earth at the edge of the road. The consequences that resulted would come later. (Here we can see the connection between the actions and the consequences, like a seed's consequence is a tree.) We could however be mistaken, writers often treat the heroes of their stories with arbitrary action in such a manner that they would not accept if the hero would be able to protest. It would be best here to show Little One's natural way of life. And that step did not have a bigger importance than drinking water. And who knows where the consequences' tree roots would branch out. The Little One was not able to protest because she was a dog, and a human word was not in her possession.

Little One was trotting, and her nose was on the grass in front of her grasshoppers, and bugs were jumping away. So she went following the scent in the grass where the cat's smell stuck to the grass' blades. If one hare would jump, she would probably run after it and forget the anger and hatred. However, the fate wrote different chapters in her life.

Sometimes the face could show up in the face of the tomcat---not even a mouse moved in midday on the slumber-dozed field. Suddenly a very strong smell hit her nose, much stranger than the tomcats. Because of that, Little One had to stop. Little One felt a knowing from the deep past, some strange and never felt fumes that were almost as unpleasant as they was inviting and taming.

Little One's heart started beating very fast. She was afraid of the unknown animal that was announcing its existence over the entire environment with an aggressive command. You could taste on the plants, on the meat, and through the smell of his sweat that this was different and much stronger than any other animal. Little One, for a moment, thought of the scent that had a similarity to the fox and the wildcat, because those were also unpleasant. However, for some incomprehensible reason, she forgave the unknown animal. She always had mood for discovery. The flame shot up in her. She could not see any enemy that could be making trouble---nowhere in sight. Little One raised her head up high. The white walls that looked like clouds under the horizon between the trees; were now clearly seen as those forming a house, with a roof made with rushes. These houses were similar to Basa's hut. Fences were made from rush that were blocking away Little One from the white walls. The tomcat's route of escape was this way. She felt his scent all the time. She did not care for the cat right now. Little One's concerns were behind a hedgerow and a smell of a certain kind of animal.

Before she jumped into the garden, she lay down flat. Probably the first law of the hunter was to look around and sniff before you start anything. Suspiciously running the rush hedge left and right, she tried to avoid surprise. Nothing moved. The wind helped her almost see inside the plant life and animals. The feeling became stranger and stranger for the presence of the mystical being. She knew that mystery was not lurking around the way those dogs that left their scent here, and even the escaped tomcat jumped over the rush hedge. And that did nothing to Little One's newest impression. From hunting, the strength of her muscles cleared the fence with ease. The reeds would not pamper or feed the weak for a long time. Next to Great Hunter or Swimmer,

Little One felt she was weak. She thought that all her enemy's strength was standard---as big as Great Hunter's strength.

If she were to run into a common village dog she would be superior not only in strength but also in smartness and wildness. Her memories were still of the brothers' hard teeth that left a deep mark on her, and in considering the dog, Little One had a great fantasia that did not bring out the dog's courage. In the garden, a fresh silky grass, and a big tree's soft shadow received her. Here and there on the ground, a green object fell down from the trees. Some fruits that she had never seen before lay there. All that, did not stop her stealth, from one bush to the other, with tight muscles, if necessary, to run or attack. Out of the shadows she stepped into the scorching sun, a black dog with thick hair came forward. The eyes could not be seen because of the long hair; however, the way it barked showed courage. It was not a big dog, so Little One was not scared. She stopped and waited. Due to the loud barking somebody stepped out of the house. At that moment, like lightening coming through, the man came out. Even if Little One had never seen one of these beings, she knew it right away.

Basa never talked about it because she did not have the knowledge of words. She became scared, and a great fright overwhelmed her. When the peasant saw the strange dog, he shouted at her with a high-pitched voice, "Where is your mother?" He bent down pretending to look for a stone, Little One did not know the movement's meaning; however, the fear from the thrown stone was inherited in the dog like the teeth in its mouth. With a dreadful scare, Little One was fleeing. Even a voice or a hand moving would scare her away, but together, the gestures were as forceful as a whip snapping against her.

The peasant laughed at the big white dog running away, like somebody put glowing embers into her. He ordered his brave house dog to be quiet and went back to the house. "What was that?" asked the wife unnecessarily because she knew what had happened by her husband's voice. It could only have been a dog. "Ah, some dog came into the garden, but not from around here. Probably belongs to the shepherds, I reckon. Luckily, it did not do damage to the ducks."

Little One ran until she reached the reeds. She was afraid to even look back. There she took a long rest and did not go back to her brothers, lurking in the thick reeds for three days, rarely eating. She was not in the mood for hunting prey. After three days, her irresistible instinct sent her way to the man. Now she could see them on the field. There were lots of them. They were swaying and bending down side by side and pulling some trees together, cutting down the dense plant-life where she had met with the tomcat. Little One would like to see the group of men up close. However, she was afraid of them. On the road, another group of people came. Little One turned away, avoiding the meeting. She cut through the field and went to the house where she had jumped into the garden before. Now she did not meet with anybody. After checking out a couple of things, she jumped over the hedge. Not a man, and not even the dog, would step forward from the house. Nobody was home.

The Little One felt it inside of her---something holding her, like a rope around her. However, she was not afraid of the feeling. There were so many known and familiar things pulling at her. She felt she belonged here and arrived from the long road, and they were waiting with her with friendly invitation. Little One ventured all the way to the white walls, and still nobody came to drive her away. By smelling, watching, and listening, her nose, eyes, and ears became acquainted with this new world. At the side of the house, she heard some noise and looked over there and saw fairly large yellow-spotted ducks shuffling forward. Little One was surprised to see they were not running away. She had lots of experience with the other family members of these ducks, the wild ones, who were very timid and careful. And when she felt a human scent on them, she was not looking for answers anymore. Little One got closer and was filled with respect toward humans with a scared feeling. She was also scared of the humans' property. The ducks were not even frightened. They were rocking in front of her nose to the well, playing in the little pond and getting dirty. Little One looked at them with amazement and did not even realize when to catch one. After that, she could not help herself but take a duck under the bush and eat it. She was looking around herself, wondering if any punishment would come to her.

Nothing moved. One duck was very little after three days of hunger. The second was an easy catch too. The man did not come forward to punish her, for Little One was waiting with a beating heart and a guilty conscience. After a while, the ducks settled down and again displayed themselves. She thought, It could be a long time before I'll see this much prey. Some faraway kid shouted. She was looking for a while and took the third duck and left for the reeds. Little One was a real sage, never letting her emotions overcome her senses.

CHAPTER 9

Swimmer could have another name, but Basa never thought it out, considering the circumstances of when she marked her puppies. It was true that Basa became a lot smarter from being around humans when she was a puppy. However, she could not grow that high in intelligence when her soul was in doubt between recollection and hesitation. After the puppies' first act of heroism, whether that be saving their own lives or when a task was much stranger than the participants themselves; the events made a mark, and so Basa gave the name Swimmer. And she never thought about it anymore. Even that marking was long obscured in her brain because of all the time she spent rearing her pups up.

Setting a forbidding example, and Basa's commands, played a big part in the growing puppies' lives and most importantly sharp teeth and strong paws were the instruments. Basa very rarely called her puppies by name in her dog language. The puppies' names would probably all be forgotten if the human whose profession it was to write down all kinds of things, and become a chronicler of the story, were to stop documenting. That's the way Swimmer stayed as Swimmer forever.

Luckily for Basa, Swimmer was not afraid of the water. However, the memory of choking in the water would be hateful to him forever. His brave escape taught Swimmer the knowledge of the slippery, cold, natural element where it was very hard to push forward. If the weather was hot outside, the water could quench your thirst. And it could cool you down in the hot summer and richly feed you. If you knew how, you could take your friends to the water and take the dangers against leach, reed-grass, and the most dangerous bottomless marsh, responsibly.

With time, it became clear that Basa's choice to name one of her puppies Swimmer proved to be the right choice. If she would have had the aptitude and hesitation and had thought about it for a long time, she would probably have called him Sullen. Swimmer was a huge dog. His legs were like columns, and he had a bear-like body with a slow-moving, slow-thinking, very stubborn mind. This type of mind could be from the bad memory of the flood, or he got it through the breeding of one of his ancestors. Since puppyhood, he rarely ever played. You could not obtain from him a tail-wagging adulation. Until the others ran freely and happily on the spring meadow grass, Swimmer lay down on a comfortable expanse of land and measured movements, looking for food. When Runner, with his crazy running, ran into Swimmer and tipped him over, Swimmer became angry and with his teeth, made Runner escape with a great howl. Even Great Hunter thought with consideration if he had to confront Swimmer. However, Great Hunter, with his great puppy strength was not afraid, even of Basa. On the other hand, Swimmer was so determined and stubborn, closing his jaw and not letting go of anything that got between its lock. The Great Hunter always had to pay a penalty for being victorious.

Swimmer did everything with principle and consistency. Swimmer's brothers probably thought of him as stupid, especially Little One. Without any fantasy, he was like a common heron. He trailed his own hunting ground with a usual habit. Swimmer stood alone--- unable to comply with the surrounding situations, or he acted like everything was going the right way. It would not matter; fire or water; his muscles just did the usual movements. That was the secret of it. Sometimes we rise to the occasion when not even Runner's impulsion or the Great Hunter's purposive bravery could handle the situation. We did not know his original characteristic for a dog in the unusual situation, but Swimmer was an extreme loner and self-centered dog.

Swimmer always went hunting and trailing alone. He never shared a prey. His thought was that the meat belonged to whoever got hold of it. That was his main philosophy, and rightly acted on it. He never gave a piece of his own prey to Little One. He ate how much he was able to, and he had a great appetite. Swimmer would bury the left-overs. Sometimes he forgot where he hid the leftovers from the other day. He would never find it once he forgot. It was not only through Swimmer's forgetfulness that the meat was lost, but due to Little One's cunning observation and stealing. That, too, was a part of the reason the food went missing. If Swimmer were to find out about Little One's cunning actions, it would be torment for Little One until she was half dead.

It would be unfair to say that Swimmer was envious. Even if he did not eat for two days, he never begged for food from his mother or brothers. He would die before asking. Swimmer had natural nobility that was not ruined by humans with dependent and servile humility, but his nature bordered more toward the wolf's unsociable endurance. In a healthy environment, when dogs are working with humans, the dogs' mental capacity will grow; however, a character with a contrasted experience (unfamiliar with human guidance), and wild genes, would become defenseless like a storm-tossed ship. What could become of the dog? A morose, false, cowardly thief. What was sadder the loss of an animal's dignity. Animals have dignity. They have muscles, health, and the power of senses- a physical intelligence. Swimmer could not have been ruined by even the worst human upbringing because even at the time of birth, his good and bad qualities were already taking shape.

Fitting his hunting style, he had a lasting hunting ground---bountiful. Missing from Swimmer's character was the pioneer's restlessness and curiosity, he was not like leaders of ancient times sniffing and leading the pack to the unknown forest. Armed with his common sense and purpose, the great wide waters, island, and marsh bogs' dotted broken line-reeds were enough---a small part of giving him enough food.

After the rest of Basa's family thoroughly finished their hunting work, Swimmer was a lost one when he turned away from the desolate and wiped-out area with slow clumsy movement. Swimmer was the first one who got into fishing. This had nothing to do with his name. It came to him by chance as the reeds' present. Swimmer was two years old when he had to move again, with the birds whistling, to find new prey. He just went with four rigid clumsy legs. He was a huge white dog with sticky, curly, gooey hair at daybreak in the sparkling light. From last year under the rancid blackening reeds broke through new reeds with a strong green color. The light breeze tried to push the little red warbler off the swaying reed. The only result was that all the animals escaped from Swimmer. They caught scent of him. Besides, Swimmer stood out of this element anyway with his furry white hair in the green plant life. He was like a stranger who didn't belong there. But somehow he figured out the order of the reeds.

Through the circle of life, the dead feeding off the living and the living feeding off the dead, through many filters, will once again connect Swimmer with the plant life's roots whenever his body would eventually die. Though, Swimmer was naturally not interested in symbiosis or the food supply principle. For him right now, the closest link in the chain to him was which animal would be willing to sacrifice itself to calm down his growing hunger. None of the animals felt it should be there responsibility. Those who had wings flew away, and those who had four legs ran away, and in a running contest, Swimmer could not give himself a lot of chances.

It was a time of nest-making, but Swimmer mingled at the wrong place in the inundating flood of the spring---where the birds would fear for their nests. The birds would rather avoid a watery place like that. Far away in the water, he saw the egrets' and heron's nests between the reeds. The big loose nests looked like they were about to fall out of the sky and get stuck between entangled reeds a couple of feet above the water. However, those nests were so far out. Even with Swimmers' determination, it would be too much to get through to them in the leech-infested thick marshy bogs.

On the dry land, if you could not reach the prey you could not eat it. Swimmer ran into a few snails. He sniffed at them and did not find them to be edible, so he went farther. The reeds were rustling a little and Swimmer stiffened up. At his legs, an angular snake head cape up with a two-pronged tongue and moved fast, exploring the road. Swimmer bent his head down to smell it. The sliding snake felt the danger and played opossum. Swimmer smelled the snake that had a cold and bad smell. It was unpleasant and really not the kind of meat he was looking for. Swimmer left the snake and went after a lapwing who shrieked around. Swimmer searched for it, wandering all over the big land.

The sun was so scorching that Swimmers' furry white hair almost caught on fire. His tongue was drooling and hanging down. He did not even realize that the meadow had been slowly changing. At that part of the growth, the steam of the marshes rotten smell disappeared. The reeds grew higher and rustled in the floating water. In the wide opening from the flood was a slow-flowing river which helped to change the reeds. Marshes and bogs, keep exchanging water side by side of the river---the river disappearing in to itself and reborn again, spreading and increasing. In some places, only the high grown reeds showed. The water here was lively, but the surface was as thick and dangerous as anywhere. Swimmer drank from the fresh water and swam through the river searching through the unknown flood.

In that area near the river, the reeds were much less. Some of the places, in the clear, shallow, water; swayed the grass and little white-and- yellow spring flowers. Above the petal heads, only the sky-blue air vibrated. Other places, according to nature's rights, had thick, dirty water; reed-rush uprooted, and there swam dead fishes and little birds that fell out from their nests.

In the shallow flat bay between the green plant life, the water was boiling and foaming and waving with a dark-copper color, like a giant unextinguished fire breaking out in the mud and hundreds of springs got pushed up to the marshy land to smooth the surface of the water. Swimmer stopped and was listening with all his senses. His weak eyes only saw the blurry, restless water. His most important spy was his nose, and that did not bring any news---only a strong, rough, fishy smell. That fish smell spread everywhere, all over the spring's flood---even at dry land, because, in the reeds,; the fish swarmed everywhere, in all kinds of variations. Lots of water birds lived there---often even four-legged predacious beasts or animals.

Here, you could find fish where nobody thought there were any. Under the marshes crusty edge, was a crying snake like mudfish in the mud. In the thick almost muddy water it was impossible to move. The stout resistant back bone of the "karasz" and gypsy fish: those fish were able to withstand hot summer when all the water disappeared, and only their backs were covered with some wet mud. The fish smell did not say too much to Swimmer, for he already knew they had existed there. However, his methodical character wished to find and check out this unusual bubbling. As he got closer, his eyes and nose started to rejoice because countless fish swirled in the water---small, big, gigantic. One over another, their backs jostled and lashed. One island of water was covered with smoky gold bodies of carps. It was spawning season.

The carps spawned here in the flat water. The fish roe and a male fish fertilized it. And millions of ball like eggs were like fish running in the water--- and if the enemy dispersed them, the fish would stop and watch like silly. A lot of them perished, and a lot more grew up for the joy of water birds and fishermen. Swimmer could not explain the occurrence. He was only interested in the food, lots of food. He was not alone in the enjoyment of the rich prey. Numberless birds were spearing, flying over, and grabbing the fish meat. The meadow eagle, fish eagle, and even the forest-living black stork showed up to this spot, grasping for the hunt. It was like the air brought news to these birds saying, "Come, lots of food here." And a bird of prey just came and plunged into the carps and, with heavy flapping wings, hit the water and lifted up the prey. The heavy fish wriggled in the eagles' claws pulling it down, hanging as it flew, until they reached dry land. Most of them liked to land right away. Those who had young birds at home carried a heavy weight. One of the eagles almost got pulled down into the water. The eagle's claws got stuck into a big heavy fish, but in the shallow water and with the countless fish, the big carp could not swim under the water or to the side for an escape. The innumerable birds, according to the birds' custom, made an infernal noise. They were not scared of Swimmer when he got closer to them. They jumped aside and scolded him. The birds' instincts were now made aware of all the dry-land animals that held their eyes on the easy water prey. Because of that, they could easily be taken out of the danger zone. Most importantly, there were so many fish that even a sharp reduction did not show up in their mighty numbers. They wouldn't be missed.

Even with all the above criteria, Swimmer ran into one animal who did not like his presence. One old gray wildcat grabbed after the fishes. When the cat saw the dog, with lightning speed, he turned around, hissed, lay flat, and moved his thick furry tail like a snake--- acting like his domesticated cousins, only much bigger and more menacing. Swimmer suspiciously watched the evil-eyed, toothed animal.

The cat scurried to the water on the bare body of Swimmer, and cut off the road to escape. He could try to snake away on the side, but with a lot of experience he knew that a quick attack was a half win. If this damn big dog was able to press him from the back when fleeing, what could the end be? Swimmer could not think over if he should attack that unpleasant animal while it was on him and cleaving his face and eyes. The cat could not really use teeth on Swimmer's furry thick hair. The dog's face was soaked with blood. Other dogs probably would have had enough already and ran away, especially when there was still a green light.

However, as we said already, Swimmer was more stubborn than a mule. He made one yap and got into a fight. He rolled to the ground and was able to rub off the cat. Compared to his clumsy move, Swimmer was on his feet with surprising speed. The cat jumped back a few feet with a warning growl. He jumped forward with two punches, and now he tried to bite. Swimmer shook him off and moved farther, not too fast and not to slow. Swimmer's face was all bloodied, and with a deep rattling growl, he did not realize it himself. Like a possessed animal, he could only see the fast-moving cat in front of him. Every other thing was squeezed out of his mind and eyes. Even the tomcat would not look at the situation lightly anymore. In the cat's long life, he had taken care of many dogs. But this one here was much bigger and had a different temperament than the others. With all the wounds Swimmer received, Swimmer still kept coming calmly ahead. If he attacked with speed, the cat could jump over the dog's head, and the dog would not be able to move fast enough to change position.

However, the tomcat knew from experience that the calmness that the dog possessed could not be played out with a couple of quick jumps. Still, the tomcat jumped forward a few times and wounded the dog, but more carefully, he stayed away and farther back. The dog's giant jaws almost grabbed his spine twice. The cat got squished fully to the edge of the water. And the dog, with its bloody head, pursued the cat. The cat now came to a point where he was compelled to jump over the attacker's head. Behind was the water— that cats do not like—and he already knew the dog was a fast swimmer and would choke him in the water.

The cat became flat. But Swimmer prevented the cat's jump. He moved first and jumped on the cat before the cat's muscle could fly him out of danger. Together, they turned into the water between the fishes, bathing in the live meat and water with a great splash and holding on to each other and fighting. The positions were changing constantly. Once the dog was over, the other time the tomcat blew the water into the air.

Shaggy white and wet gray hair got mixed with the fishes' golden bodies. The carps did not care about the fight in their ecstatic spawn. It was like the other two were dancing their own fertility water dance. And they got deeper into the water free of the fish bodies, trying to kill one another. They went under and came back up again. The cat rode halfway on top of the dog's back with a satanic face, and again they ducked under the water for a while. They stayed under the surface. It seemed like they wanted to deceive whoever their audience could be. Which one was going to stay alive? But they came up entangled again, except now Swimmer was on top. Again, they now went under the water for the third time.

The stirring water slowly became smooth, and not one of them came up. Finally Swimmer came out alone, and the wild cat could not be seen anymore. Swimmer climbed out to the shore. The oozing blood made his furry hair rose-tinted like a marble grain. He shook himself and looked around to see if the cat came out. But he did not. He calmly went to the smarming fishes, stepped into the shallow water, and took one of the big-sized carps out. Then he lay flat on his stomach over the wriggling fish while the fish's tail was hitting his side. He did not give attention to the fish and only wanted to rest. After a while, he raked the fish from under his belly, and for a test bite, he sunk his teeth into the fish.

Swimmer did not have the habit of making a big fuss about his heroism or his wounds. Swimmer had been hungry since morning and he wanted to eat and did not see any reason why he should not. It was enough for him that nobody stood in between he and his food; and that he was the one who was still alive.

Swimmer would not be surprised if somebody encouraged him to brag, or give in because of his wounds. As I had said earlier, Swimmer had a very limited fantasy life. He did not care for the past or the future, not even as little as a dog could. Swimmer was a narrow minded realist. To him, only the present and the facts of material proof could guide him into his actions. After the incident with the wild cat, nobody would stand up and veto his right to the spawning fish realm. Swimmer met with only one Other who thought better of it to run away through his den holes out on to the dry land. So Swimmer stayed as the only four legged animal that was able to claim customary duty over the fish. The customary tariff was only for a short time, as the fish spawn would surely end. He could only find a few fish, but since the stupor was gone, they escaped the moment that they saw his shadow in the water.

It looked as though the fish had disappeared from the flat water forever. Swimmer did not need any more proof and looked sadly at the small fishes as they flashed their shiny, silvery sides in the warm muddied water. Swimmer turned around and left for the meadow's unknown area, leaving the vanished fish-spawning place for good. He headed toward where it seemed like a narrow main-road canal, with a slowly gurgling and bubbling river remained at its side.

In reality, that was a real highway for people in a rush. This was a roadway for people who knew the reeds and the water well. They went by boat from one village to the other because they did not have a road on dry land. Whoever took a chance in the water and unknowingly ventured on---even their bones could not be found by the people of the meadows—fishermen, and shepherds. The bending river was covered with rushes as the waves slowly floated and carried the weight of water lilies and wild ducks. From the reeds, a water hen sailed out, and the water snake rippled through with a waving movement on the narrow waterway.

Still, Swimmer could not catch anything. He even tried his best at sneaking around, but alas, there was no prey. All of the prey had escaped already, scantily jumping away to the deep places. His attention was occupied by the danger of his road, and he could not hear the water bubbling in front of the boat. He only came to his senses when he heard a giant booming and felt a strange hit. With a cry, he turned around and broke and crushed the reeds, escaping from the unseen enemy. One of Swimmer's hind legs was hit by chopped lead.

Swimmer could not feel his leg. It was like pulling a stiff clump after him, hanging lamely. Blood was pouring out. He snapped at it to take away the unknown feeling, but he could find nothing. In the flat-bottomed black boat, two men were sitting. On one of the man's hands, a big shapeless rifle was still smoking, while the other man paddled quietly. "You have had it, ugly vermin", said the man who held the rifle. He was the one who took the fish, not a fox. "Who could be the owner?" referring to Swimmer, asked the paddling old man. His face was fully wrinkled and had deeply sitting dust in the skin that broke through like black scarred lines. The fisherman pointed back toward an uncertain way and thought of the godless shepherds. The shepherds had a bad reputation. It was much to be regretted.

"Beautiful dog", mumbled the old man and pulled one stroke. He lifted the paddle out of the water and looked at the water's shining rainbow. "And you, why are you sorry for it?" snarled the younger man like an old woman. "Dog, dog! There are a lot of them around. Look how much I lost because of the dog. You live on the benefit of the fish, so why are you crying?"

"Because it was a beautiful dog, for a watchdog around the house, "said the old man, and he was afraid to say more because he lived in the same hut with his daughter and her husband. The fisherman would throw him out because of the dog.

Still thinking to himself, It was a nice dog. Would be nice if that small peasant cottage could watch over that nice dog, and that he wouldn't be among the ugly wet meadows with leeches, all the time. He told his daughter to marry a peasant, not a vagrant. But you could talk your heart out. The fisherman still mumbling, "I have lost one round of gunpowder. To buy one round of gun powder would take away lots of fish. Luckily, this dog would not steal anymore fish."

Swimmer hardly dragged his legs. He did not know who inflicted his wound, but in his escape, he saw the people and recognized them; even if it was the first time he had seen a human. The human was like a wild animal when they first met the dog and concurred they recognized him right away, especially where the humans lived. Who was this big fearful beast of prey? Better to get out of the way and run the minute his scent reached your nose, because it was worse than the reeds' bushfire and a flood of icy water. Swimmer was reassured that it was unavoidable.

Swimmer did not know if he got punished for being a fox or a stray dog. Wherever he went, a dripping blood left a mark on the grass and reed-rushes. After a while, he could not hold himself and lay down on the thick bushy willows, licking his wound. So far, his leg was insensible and stiffening from the hard hit, and now the inflammation started. He felt fire glow in his throbbing wound. With difficulty, he dragged himself to the water and drank. After his head fell to shore, his nose splashed by the undulating water. For two nights and two days, he lay in the bushy willow with traumatic fever and was silent and unmoved by the tormenting agony. A fox barked and an owl screeched at night, adding to his suffering, and it made him a real beast of prey. He learned how it felt to be left alone, and how it was to be afraid of man.

By the third daybreak, he tried to stand up. His legs were shaking and bending under him from the loss of blood, and his hunger. Even though Swimmer was thin, his body could not hold him. He needed to take a few steps to teach his muscles how to do the trade of walking. He left his bloody, dirty wound bed, continuously hiding and concealing himself according to the ancient blood laws. On the rush was an incubating wolf's scent. Swimmers' hair stood up. The scent was a cold old trace, not a signal for danger. No threatening menace stood over the blue sky and green rush's peaceful tranquility. Before Swimmer was able to reach his home, he had to test himself again. Basa's litter was given by fate. Even the small things, like following their mother's route, were given to them by fate. The puppies' instincts were complete, and they were doing what Basa was afraid to do or as fate ordered otherwise.

Swimmer took a long time to reach the communal den. His own scent became cold by the time he recovered from his sickbed. He did not know which way to go. To stand in one place would be useless, so he started to go up toward the riverside. The night came on him, and his stomach demanded food; but he was too tired and weak to hunt. He lay down tired and weak on a bunch of dry reeds. At that moment on the other side of the reeds, a wounded heron, who disturbed Swimmer, tried to escape with a shot-through broken leg and wing, but after a few steps, sat down with a weapon-like beak held against Swimmer. The two animals, which were wounded by humans, looked at each other. And Swimmer finished what his mother failed to do. Even in his weakness, he was able to kill the silvery bird. He ate the birds even though they were a leathery and fishy-smelly meat.

The next day, he heard a dog barking that the wind brought to him. Runner was chasing some game. Swimmer found his home. Not one of his family members was surprised by Swimmer's turning up. Only Basa displayed excitement as she rejoiced; because to her, each one of them was dear, even when they were already grown-ups. Basa tried to lick clean Swimmer's bloody wound and furry hair. She left him alone afterward, and did not care about her limping son anymore. Swimmer went to find and eat all kinds of bitter grass and lay down. Within a few days, his wound cleared, but when the forecast changed and the storm neared all night. He could not sleep. His wound bothered him, and his hind leg scraped the ground. It was like trying to escape from a trap. Through his wound he became knowledgeable of the forecast and paid value only to it. He never called the attention of is family members, not just because the dog was not able to clearly communicate a complicated situation like this. However, his principle was "you should be smart for yourself".

CHAPTER 10

RUNNER

To first glance at Runner would not show you much of him. He was a big white kuvasz dog, probably thinner at his flank or smaller at the back. The wolf blood hid in him so well, and you could believe that his slenderness looked rather famished. His legs did not grow as long as a greyhound. Great Hunter carried his body high above the ground, as high as Runner.

Of course, both of them had long legs, especially next to the bear-looking Swimmer and the stunted Little One. Runner's appearance did not show his most valued characteristic---his speediness. Somewhere in Runners' muscles, flesh, joints, and bones lie hidden and unnoticed that quick power that made him fly faster than the fastest hare. (It is not by chance that we called Runner's speediness a "feature trait" and not a quality or virtue.)

Like some of the literary figures, Runner's state of being was guided by only one quality. He knew about himself. He was fast, faster than any animal that lived in the marshland. And in his swagger was the speediness that he fondled and trusted in himself. This fully suited his pleasure. All the other qualities in capturing prey---cunning, observation, and patience---were entirely missing features in Runner's character. With his nose catching the trace of scent, with his fast legs running until he caught his prey, with great snapping jaws---that was all Runner's knowledge and thus he was happy in the marsh, rushing to many brooks, ponds, marshlands, and bog-swamps.

Most of the time, he could not successfully pursue his prey by running them down. For that reason, sometimes he went out of the reeds, and at the edge of the reeds where there were wet grass meadows—he would stalk his prey, where there were obstacles—the brooks and creeks helped runner, stopping the escaping prey. Runner flew over the obstacles like a bird, with a dog's character, even with limited consistency—he would like to take his prey that he caught in the reeds to the grassy meadow and let it go, so he would be able to catch it again with his speedy running. This reasoning power, with a little exaggeration, could be called mostly a virtue, or we could sometimes call it stupidity. The truth in all this—only in literary work—is where and when you are able to find it. Little One, however, called Runner stupid and not because she was smaller and weaker. Runner was constantly offended by it, but it still had some truth to it. And that always showed Little One's discernment. Hares that lived in the marshy reed were called rush-hares. They are more talented than their cousin on the fields. In the rush, there were lots of hiding places, but more constant enemies. With these two conditions, they always became more skillful than their cousins.

Little One quickly came to know the rush-hare. It was mostly out of play or out of passion for hunting that made her go after them without any hope of success. She could eat hare meat only when the mother hare gave birth to the litter. That is when Little One was able to satisfy her hunger for hare meat. She became so fond of the young hare's meat that she learned a couple of tricks of the mother hare's habits. When the hare's litters were growing and even when they were getting bigger, the mother was suckling the young hares once a day. On that occasion, the mother hare clapped her ear to call for the young ones who were hiding. Little One, with a soul of a fox, listened all the time to the noise of the reeds where the hare's clapping ears were heard. Little One would almost surely come around within a short while.

Swimmer never cared for hare. It would be a great opportunity if he would go after an injured hare. Even Great Hunter did not like to go after a hare. He regretted the exhausting time it took. Great Hunter had different tricks that brought the soft furry prey to his mouth; sneak at them against the winds, grab them on the tail, or push them against the water. Those things were more fitting for Great Hunter's mood if he ever wanted to catch hare.

For Runner, it was a self-amusement to run after hare. In that mad manner and the way the grass scurried under his feet or between bushes, a hare ran in zigzags with a stretched body and flat ears to be able to save its skin. All of that was a play to Runner. It was a delight to feel his own lightness and stamina, and the ecstasy of the race.

However, hare hunting did not only entail running like a mad dog. The older hares, quite a few times, made Runner look silly until it came to Runner cutting off their winding method, able to catch them at full speed. While the hare jumped to the side, Runner did not lose any extra time in biting them because then only a choking handful of hair could be left in the hunters's mouth, and the plucked out hare would escape.

Runner became a master of hare hunting. When he reached his prey with a light move of his head, he flung the prey up in the air, and when it fell down, he grabbed it by the spine. Sometimes, he caught more than a few hares in one hunting day. At this time, he grinned with happiness, with a crazy wriggle in his back. He hid the leftover and extra prey all the time, even what the arrogant Great Hunter left. Runner constantly was afraid and was getting ready for a great famine. The places where he was hiding his prey were unaccounted for. And he looked for those hiding places very rarely because he liked fresh meat much better. That is how the marsh insects and vermin became the feeding alternative for Runner.

Ever predacious animal caught prey by their own means. Runner learned very quickly that he had unnatural speed, and if he could not catch hare, the uncountable water birds gave him an easy prey for his hungry stomach. He put all his confidence into his speed. The wild duck looked clumsy when taking off from the water, and moved with difficulty, tapping on the water with his flat feet before catching flight with its wings. That was enough for the slender white body of Runner to fly through the air and catch the heavy fat bird. Before all that, Runner needed to learn a few general things about the wild ducks: the pochard type of duck did not fly away, they ducked underwater and swam away.

Runner, all wet with frustration, had to climb to the shore. He enjoyed a great deal of bathing. He learned he could take a prey out of the duck family—even the ducks that were underwater— because their tail feathers were sticking above the water. Capturing ducks is what we called Runner's knowledge and pastime hobby. Surprisingly, the danger did not come from his delighted pastime hobby. However, it came from the wrathful autumn.

This upcoming autumn was Runner's second time experiencing the season in his life, and it slowly slipped into winter. The water lilies shallow flat leafage went underwater as the reed-grass turned to deathly yellow, and the tip of the reads; the black flog, turned to light brown and became tattered. The migrating birds left a long time ago, and other roaming birds from the north came to the empty place. The great swamp became quiet. On the proceeding reed, only sparrows carping on the dry rush leaves stopped for rest. Toward evening, the wild geese came back home with a great V sign in the air, breaking up smaller and smaller wedges over the reeds.

In the thick heavy fog, the low-flying geese looked like phantoms. The fish were clamped together as deep as a two-yard column. The pike were lurking in the corner of the rush. With a gray-marble body and duck-face teeth, the ducks were as big as locust tree thorns. Some were moving in the condition of a bleak stupor, in the crystal clear, cold, frosty water. The reeds hardly breathed, and the open water still freely quivered. On the following days, cold wind came and pushed the water waves on the reeds and they became as frosted as small ice necklaces. The next day, all the reeds wore a crystal necktie a few inches above the calmed-down water. Runner did not like the winter. He still remembered from last winter how the crusty snow broke under him and wounded his legs. The treacherous frosty ground toppled him over when he ran. The dangerous deep marshland was covered with snow. The prey became fewer, and the young hares were more agile. He was happy for the calm weather that came after the ice-cold wind. Even the sun still choked in the thick fog. With Little One, she and Runner started on to the grass meadow, but at the edge of the reeds, Runner stopped and with disdain watched Little One who went toward the grass meadow without precaution. Runner did not know that Little One already knew the road with experience. With great patience and a piece of cunning, she had to be careful around the house where she wanted to steal some chickens, eggs, and milk. Runner waited until his sister disappeared into the fog. Afterward, he put his nose to the ground and ran for a while by the reeds. He wanted to find out what came out and what went into the reeds. At first he found a fox's scent already cold, but Runner had the knowledge to know something about the fox: was he creeping into the reeds with a full stomach? If he was not that hungry, he would probably go after him and rumple at the red fur a little bit. Farther up, a parade of cock-pheasants jumped in front of him, and he found a few hare tracks, but all this went into the reeds. Runner was very hungry. The reeds quickly closed him out of his food resources. He went farther to the edge of the reeds. He stopped at once like a hunting dog who felt the prey. The smell of skunk that hit his nose already left the reeds.

However, the track was still hot. For a long time, he wanted to settle an account with a skunk that went back to early summer, when the skunk disgracefully threatened him. Both of them hunted for little birds. The skunk came with the wind, and Runner, who first noticed the skunk, stepped in front of the smelly creature. It did not matter how big Runner was. He was still a clumsy, foolish puppy dog who would like to observe closer that wicked-looking dark haired animal. He did not have a purpose of hostility

He stepped in front of the skunk with curiosity and a little playfulness. In any case, he wanted to examine the short-legged, thick-furred animal and would decide after whether he would attack it, run away, or play with it. The animal's smell was not encouraging, but that did not stop his first superficial impression. The skunk came to its senses only when the big white dog stood in front of it. It already knew Runner's breed, and they were a deadly enemy: to turn around to flee would be deadly to the skunk. So the skunk attacked first.

Runner was still not on his guard when the ugly creature bit into the bottom of his mouth. When Runner tried to rub on the ground to get himself free from the vicious animal, it jumped away and sprayed him with some terrible-smelling liquid. Runner, now half blind, cried with a high-pitched voice and turned himself around on the ground. When his eyesight became clear, he wanted to kill the skunk, who was already far away. And what was more, the terrible smell ate into his fur and he could not get it out. He tried rubbing it off on the grass and washing it out with the water. When he got home, he went to his mother to complain. She, with a wild tooth, snapped and chased him away. The brothers and sister, with fur standing up on their necks, were biting after him. Runner could not stay in the hut. For one week, he stayed in the reeds until the smell disappeared from his furry hair.

With a submissive repentance afterwards, he was able to come back to the others. From this day on, Runner had a deadly hatred towards skunks. And now he found one of their tracks. His neck's hair stood up, and his teeth showed, and he growled loudly. Another dog would probably put aside his hatred until his stomach was filled, but Runner inherited his mother's stubbornness—not on the scale of Swimmer—but still, his hunger flew him into a rage. And with a trailing wolfish run, he started to go after the skunk.

The skunk left the reeds to go to its usual winter shelter, to the houses where the humans lived. The skunk was looking for a wood stack or some corner of a roof or any hiding place for the winter time. A place around small livestock where it would be easier to get through the winter until spring, rather than out in the frosty reeds, would be good. Of course, Runner did not know this. With his speedy running, he came very close to the skunk; in his thoughts, they should meet at any moment. What Runner could not comprehend was why the skunk wandered this far from the reeds? When here there was less food than in the reeds. Finally Runner reached a high fence of a wooden plank. The skunk was at the bottom of the plank and squeezing through a small hole; he felt the skunk's deep smell. Where a skunk was able to slip through, a big dog like Runner was unable to get through for sure.

Runner was running left and right and at the side of the fence, but that never ended. To make a big hole bigger and wider would be too much work for his legs, especially with his eagerness. In his feverous irritation, he whimpered in a low voice and scratched on the plank of the fence. And in a moment of time, he ran back; and with one sweep forward, partly flying and scrawling, fell over the high fence. Anybody who could see that jump would be amazed by the sight. However, Runner did not know, until now, how to measure his own capacities. And with any swagger and a little numbness in his legs, he went to pick up the skunk's trail. The skunk found a shelter in the ice-pit covered with a thatched reed hut. It was a familiar hut to the dog; it was made out of rush and resembled where they had a den.

However, certain unknown smells and his instinct told him to be cautious. That unknown smell, even though he had never met with it, gave him the same unaccountable feeling that was repulsive and still attractive---just like Little One's feeling about that same scent from before. Something broke up inside of him; his stomach became heavy as if he drank too much, but at the same time he felt thirsty too. Runner would not know what he was reminiscing about, but even if he knew, he would not comprehend a thing. Because, it was not he who remembered or recollected, but it was his mother and his shepherd-dog ancestors.

Runner's thoughts ran through him with a shudder and vanished. The unknown beings made him cautious until he discovered the hole where the skunk hid inside of. He became enraged and savagely started tearing down the reed wall with his mouth and legs. The dry reed stuck to his tongue and to the roof of his mouth. At times he sniffled into the hole and knew the skunk was still lurking somewhere. After some time, Runner realized that the skunk was not in the wall of reeds anymore; it had escaped into the hut that was covering the ice-pit. Runner ran over there and sniffed inside.

A cold air hit him. Faintly feeling the unknown being was not in the hut. However, he still felt that the skunk was hiding somewhere inside. So Runner jumped into the dark. Between jumps he felt it; a danger came to visit him. But he was unable to stop midair, and a jump felt like it would never end. Runner lunged and lunged and with a big thump, hit the ground stretched out. For a few minutes, he lay down without moving as the life left his body. And his head jerked and his legs followed. He still lay for a while and turned over to his stomach with difficulty. His whole body ached; he felt like every bone in his body had cracked. He tried to stand up. It was successful. All his body parts were moving.

The pain left his body very slowly. He instinctively sat down to not strain himself. For Runner's luck, the ice-pit was empty; the fresh new ice could not be cut yet. If the ice in the pit had already been cut, Runner probably would not have fallen so hard. At the same time, the hard ice could injure him worse than to lay between big chunks of ice that even to the thick-haired kuvasz-dog would be a frosty day. Finally, he felt strong enough to escape. From the bottom of the ice-pit, he could see the daylight even if the light only broke through the door dimly.

The ice-pit was about four yards deep; to fall from that height, Runner could come off badly if the dry straw covering the ice had not been left behind on the bottom. Runner went around the walls to see if he could find some way to climb out, but the walls were very smooth; he was unable to grab on. The ladder that was used to get the ice to lie across the ice-pit's wall's edge, Runner, of course, did not know what that was for. The wood was unknown to him, but even if he knew, it would not matter, because it could not be used by him. He gathered up all his strength and jumped. It was a huge jump, but he still could not reach the pits' edge. He tried again and fell back. He became terrified, and, with a maddening jump broke his nose. His mouth was filled with dirt; his claws broke down. The blood mixed with dirt, and wet clay was glued to his paws. He was afraid to even howl in his near craziness. For that he was too much of a wild animal.

It was getting dark in the ice-pit, and Runner had reached his limit. He became deadly tired and was only able to lie on the straw. That dreadful pitfall slowly killed his will to live. He did not have the energy left to fight; it was an incomprehensible place, and fear blocked his ability to adapt. If only one mouse, a mole, or even a piece of meat would crawl into his trap for him to eat. In Runner's body, the hunger came forward; and with a hunger, his will to live came back. But underneath this damp mildew straw, only a flat millipede and a pasty-looking worm stirred. Runner felt that he had to die here.

At night, there was once a time when the raging anger came back to him, and he beat himself in the darkness. At daybreak, on the first light, he was half dead and stretched-out on the straw. Before noon, the entry door of the ice pit got blocked from the light and it became dark in the pit. Runner knew some unknown beings were about to come, those whose smell he felt by him all the time; there was a woman and a man talking.

"John, make sure somebody is going to go clean out the ice-pit. Last year the straw was already rotten when we put the meat in, and I picked up the smell. I did not like to see the confusion when everyone was putting the ice into the pit. And who knows, a dead mouse or even a cat could be in there."

"Yes the way you ordered it missus", answered a deep voice.

Runner, who had still never met a human before, was able to distinguish between the two. Not only that one of them was a man and the other was a woman, but that the person with the piping thin voice was the more important person. Runner was already becoming restless; he wanted to fight with those who held him in the trap. Even the knowledge that he was afraid of them, he menacingly started to growl. Now they heard him. "Ha. Something is growling down there." John said. The woman with a little nervous voice said, "Silent." Runner was still growling. And a deep voice said, "Could be some animal, maybe a wolf".

"A wolf? At this time wolves do not come around. Could be the Tisza dog that disappeared last week. Go down and take a look! Get a lamp.

"A lamp, what for?"

"I am telling you that was Tisza. I am sure it was so hungry that it was unable to howl anymore. Go start!"

Above Runner's head, John pulled the strange big wood and threw it down close to him; he needed it to jump away. After one unknown started to step down the ladder, he had a fearful and unpleasant smell that he never felt before. A dog, which grew up around humans, would know that smell of tobacco, steam of plum brandy, and rancid lard smell. Runner was trembling and ready to fight. The man came down slowly, looked down, and saw the white dog and called, "Tisza, you! Stay Tisza, come, and do not be afraid. Enough of this growling. Tisza!"

When he reached the bottom of the ladder, he stepped aside a little bit. Runner's will to fight was over. He was afraid. In his fear, he found the escape route like a fleeing cat. He flew by the man who sprang back on to the ladder. In a normal situation, he would not have been able to go up on the tricky steps, or he would still be very slow. Now, he slipped and beat his legs with the ladder, but he was already up. By the time the bailiff of the estate realized what was going on, Runner pushed aside the woman on his route and ran away.

Not one of them could say a word due to their amazement. "That was not a Tisza", the bailiff said finally. "No. Never saw a big dog like that. How did it come around?" The bailiff climbed up the ladder. I am sure; the dog felt the meat smell that was here during the summer. And was hungry and wanted to eat. He could be right, permitted the woman.

"Make sure to clean the pit, and close the door."

While Runner ran like someone who had lost their head, some unnamed fear ran through his whole body. All his senses, his brain, and his instinct stopped working. At first, he got through some wooden fences and found himself between giant animals that were more afraid of him than Runner was of them. They stomped their legs and lashed their tails. One of the bigger animals lashed out at Runner with his front leg, because he could not hit him while Runner ran to bite him with big yellow teeth. The animals were whining, the men were shouting. Runner was happy to come out from the trap without injury.

Now, he was running between the houses, geese; the ducks and chickens that were running away in front of him. The men were running out of the houses with broomsticks and pitchforks. Runner hid under the carriages and behind pigsties and drinking troughs; and he tried to escape. From everywhere and all over, the hunting pack could be heard. All the dogs of all the houses came together at once and chased the escaping Runner, who with lightning speed passed by a big round skirted woman who threw a bucket of water at him. He avoided two men with a pitchfork and ran into a pigsty. The dogs ran after him. Runner ran and stopped at an obstacle that was in front of him. It was a pigsty. He found himself at a dead end. The dogs were onto him already, tearing into him and grabbing his furry hair. Runner was overcome by a deadly wolf's anger. He did not want to escape anymore, but to kill. Get revenge. With bloodshot eyes, he turned on to one of the rich vizsla dogs. The vizsla ran backward, with a torn up nose. Runner at once became calm like a genuine fighter. This was not the invulnerable lifeless ice-pit, and it was not even the unknown being who gave him a strange feeling. Those were dogs that still belonged to the unknown being, but Runner was not scared of dogs. It looked like the more dangerous dog was the dachshund. The others tore and bit into Runner; his back was covered with blood. But the cunning dachshund was an old fox killer; he did not waste time on the furry thick hair. First of all, he bit Runners' first leg, unable to use it, and pushed himself forward to the soft unprotected stomach. Runner did not waste his time to get in a deep bite. Whit his huge head and with one move, he threw the dachshund into the air, like he used to with a hare, and when it fell down, he grabbed it by the spine. He bit only once, but when he let loose, the short-legged dog, was lifeless.

By this time, the people reached the lifeless dog. Runner, considering he was a young dog, acted wisely like an old wolf until that time; now he showed his knowledge to the dogs who were accustomed to living with a man. He was quickly biting back two times, and the two dogs who grabbed into him howled up, which showed to them what an excellent hunter Runner was in the reeds.

And he started off against the people. With all hope, he would not be able to escape from so many men with weapons. Then a woman in the back screamed out loud "Oh dear! It is mad!" In the next moment, everybody ran away with loud screams. Every predacious animal, even those who grew up around houses, had an instinct to go after who ran or fled. Runner would probably have done the same for his own distraction had the last one and a half days did not disturbed him so badly. So because of that, he just ran on his track where the two already torn up dogs were until he found a gate where the two dogs stopped. Better not to start a fight with a huge kuvasz in strange territory.

They gave him a brave bark until he disappeared into the far distance. That is how Runner met with humans for the first time. If he knew how to speak, he could exchange his experience with Little One and Swimmer, and probably could have some explanation from Basa; but the dog communication that was manifest was exceeded by the complicated story. The experience probably did not trouble him, because he was unable to talk it out. By the time Runner reached the reeds, he was calm enough to find one of the prey that he was hiding. Basa felt where Runner could have been with his torn up body. Sometimes Runner was agonizing in his dream, whimpering and struggling as if he wanted to free himself. Only Basa suspected that her son became involved with a human. Even a fading memory was enough for her to not let Runner go to the meadow grass anymore where the roads lead to the humans.

CHAPTER 11

GREAT HUNTER

Nobody would believe such a thing that Great Hunter was the brother of the other three white-haired dogs. At first glance, he showed the genuine wolf look: a huge forest wolf; however, a giant like him was very rare in wolves. He was light gray, and the temple of his head was flat and his ears were much bigger and pointer than his mother's. His coarse hair was not sleek and did not converge into a soft waving line as a white kuvasz's hair would. But one attentive observer could recognize the heritage of the mother; an enormous chest and a strong muscled thick neck. Also, he had a more angular nose than a wolf has. Great Hunter never met an observer; no one knew if it was by chance or by his characteristic structure's inevitable result. Out of the four family members, he was the only one who never met a human in his lonesome roaming. Later in a collective hunting, he met with a commander but we will give the account later in its own place.

To have given Great Hunter a different name would have been a mistake. Basa giving him the name of Great Hunter was an excellent decision. The hunting and catching of prey was in his blood. And nobody was able to adapt to the situation and change of plans, for he was an animal who aimed the mark. He was able to crawl silently like a snake just to eat a mouth of full field moles: he was capable of staying silently and unmoved for hours just to catch a young coot. However, if the situation called for it, he could run the hare until the hare dropped dead as Runner would do. Just like Little One, he stole the eggs from the dangerous birds that had beaks like a spear. At springtime, in the flat shallow water; the spawning fish were in danger by the Great Hunter. He was fishing like a cat; his giant teeth caught the spawning carp out of the water so efficiently, as a cat would do with its claws.

In Great Hunter, the father wolf's cunning ability and the mother dog's intelligence and power mixed in him enormously out of the four puppies. By the time he was three years old, he became so strong that he would be able to bring down a hind. But the hind very rarely came to the reeds. And it was not assured that Great Hunter would try risking his power against a big unknown animal. With Great Hunter, it was hard to make a guess because bravery and fighting spirit were in his veins, aside from his swaggering self-confidence. With those qualities, and with his powers, he was tyrannical over his big brothers, who were less powerful than he. He made the best place in the den for himself.

At summer on the island, he liked to sleep under the willow bush; when any of his brothers came too close to where he rested, he attacked them with deadly rage. He merely just picked a quarrel. He beat Runner away from his own food. He never touched Swimmer's food because he was afraid of Swimmer; he knew Swimmer did not know how to play or joke. If they picked a quarrel, one of them would lose, and the loser would stay on the ground forever. He even picked a fight with a stubborn Basa who had authoritarianism over them. Basa came home without prey, and she felt deserving to get a share from her wolf-son's meat-prey. Great Hunter's eyes were flashing; baring his teeth was his way of receiving his mother. Basa tried to use her power, the right of a mother; Great Hunter began to fight like crazy. Basa felt, for the first time in her life, that a stronger animal put her shamefully in flight.

Little One was the only individual who could get away with

almost everything against Great Hunter. With playful smirking and playing a clown to take away the food, she sometimes grasped into Great Hunter so hard that the blood showed under Little One's tooth. And all of that, Great Hunter endured, with patience and submission. With her cowardly malevolence, Little One took advantage of Great Hunter's affections. She demanded to be served with the prey Great Hunter caught, and she played up to his sensitive and touchy mood. She found a safe haven behind Great Hunter when her two brothers tried to punish her for stealing. However, with her sensitivity, she knew when to stop all the time. She was afraid to excessively irritate Great Hunter. Little One, with her domination, sometimes brought some good food to the whole gang. On the freezing lifeless days when nobody was able to catch any prey except Great Hunter, he was willing to share his prey with the others just to make Little One happy. One more thing that made Little One useful to the family: she was the spy of Great Hunter, who liked to prowl even though she was not as purposeful of an observer as Great Hunter, who knew everything about his prey's character. What kind of knowledge was needed, to know how to catch some things? Nevertheless, Little One very smartly gave a report of what was going on in the reeds with her limited dog communication. One time when Great Hunter went to select a prey and between a change of wind or the distance of the marshy bog swamp prey between him and his prey, he went back to his willow bush to sleep. This time Little One was completely stunned and walked uneasily after Great Hunter for two days with a great adulation, looking for her strong brother's better mood. She had found a roebuck for Great Hunter. The roebuck was young; he grew only one horn of is antlers, and he carried it with pride. It was still soft and white. The new horn donned a velvety cover. The young roebuck could not wait until he was able to rub off his soft horn on the young tree's trunk on this beautiful morning. He felt that the whole world belonged to him. He was grazing on a grassy little sand-hill and often looked at himself in the still water, and in his joy, he jumped up and down; which would suite a young goat more, but not a roebuck who was trying to protect his manhood.

That is how Little One found him. For a while, she was taking pleasure to just look at the roebuck flattening down behind a bunch of tied rush. However, she was not taking pleasure in the roebuck's gracefulness; she was looking at a lot of meat. She was in the mood to attack the roebuck by herself, but the velvet-looking soft antler and the size of the live meat restrained her. The Great Hunter! She thought to herself that she was happy with the decision to share because she liked to do favors. She wanted to sneak away carefully, but the roebuck could hear something. It jumped and ran into the reeds. Even faraway, the roebuck's alarming bark could be heard. Little One was not sorry for the roebuck that got away, because it was too late in the morning and there would not be enough time to reach it anyway. The deer liked to use the spots that they had used before, so Little One thought that he would be back by sundown.

Great Hunter was sleeping under his own willow-bush when Little One found him. She did not go near to him; she tried to wake him in his sleep once before. She learned that if you wake the Great Hunter, he first bit and looked at who he was dealing with only afterward. With a respectful distance, she lay down and took a nap. That is how she waited for her gray brother to wake up. Great Hunter finally stretched out, turned around on his back yawning once and clinked his teeth. He was not finished with his awakening ceremony as he stood on his legs and stretched again, two front legs stuck forward with a slight angle-- pushing down his chest to the ground. With his body on an incline, he got rid of his muscle faintness.

Little One was patient and waited out to call the attention of her brother with a low bark. She did not go near to him because an awakening Great Hunter was morose and provocative. And Little One, the tyrant, felt this time it would be better to wait. She had no power over Great Hunter in that state of mood. With sluggish moves, Great Hunter moved forward.

Now, Little One went to Great Hunter and danced around with excitement, barking and whimpering in any way, trying to give him a great deal of important information about the fact that she saw meat---a lot of meat. Great Hunter had the habit of only going hunting when he was hungry. He still felt the prey from that morning in his belly, so he sat down and started to scratch himself.

Little One became angry and started poking and biting Great Hunter's shoulder repeatedly. He took her gestures with indifference and mused on her aggressiveness. Nobody in the reeds had as much patience as Great Hunter, when patience was called for. He just scratched himself and went back to sleep. Little One continued again. Out of Little One's report, Great Hunter had a suspicion that there was some big prey out there. However, only those suffering from stupidity would hunt in midday during springtime. Only the scatterbrained Runner, living for his own amusement, with his tongue hanging out behind the running hare— the starved or the hungry— hunted at this time. Great Hunter's movements were always guided by practicality except during a fight. But, now, with his full stomach, he did not want to fight. Fighting with an empty stomach added more fuel to the fighting spirit. He woke up by nightfall, freshly hungry, with eager attention.

By this time, Little One had come back from her unsuccessful bird hunt. Now she needed to hurry and lift her legs up faster to avoid Great Hunter's bites. With a rapid trot leading to the opening where the roebuck was expected to appear, Great Hunter hid behind a bush against the wind. With gnashing teeth, he sent Little One back. At this time, he would not play a joke. The roebuck came at dusk. As Little One suspected, that was the roebuck's permanent return point from exiting the reeds. Until then, not one predacious animal bothered him. Still, the roebuck stood with suspicion for a long time between the standing long reeds before it stepped out from their protection. He did not feel anything aside from the rush of a thousand merging leaves, the smell of it too, and did not hear anything except the night's usual low but still, alarm noises.

The roebuck stepped out of the opening. An unknown danger was hidden from his senses. Often lifting his head up to pry into the air, then jumping like something scared him, he grazed while being highly alarmed. The roebuck was so alarmed, that Great Hunter, who was behind the bush, was afraid to budge. The young buck, so proud of his manhood, already had his fate written down. His faith, with slow grazing and walking, sent him to the willow bush, where the unknown fear went through him. By this time it was too late. A big, dim, shadow with the force of Great Hunter's body behind it went for the roebuck's throat. The roebuck went down and buckled his legs from the great weight. He successfully jumped up; but Great Hunter hung at his throat and, with his front legs and strong claws. tore up the front of the buck.

Great Hunter's victim carried him to the wall of the reeds. As the killer hung from the roebuck's neck, his teeth reached the main artery and the roebuck fell down. He still kicked once or twice, while Great Hunter began to open up his prey's body. Of course, Little One showed up, who sat comfortably behind the bush as the battle had started. Now, she came forward to seize her share, as part of the intelligence service. She waited until Great Hunter tore up the deer's belly and with her tyranny drove away her stronger brother. And by herself, she started to eat the warm soft bowel parts. Great Hunter was waiting as a meek guard on duty until Little One filled her stomach. With a generous spirit she led him back to the fresh meat. The roebuck was Great Hunter's first big prey; he became more courageous and fearless. For a long time, he did not encounter any animals that he would shrink from. Bringing down the roebuck was his real initiation into becoming a wild beast forever.

Swimmer and Great Hunter achieved Basa's faith in them; they had already done something that Basa was unable or afraid to do. It would be a mistake to believe that Great Hunter was gone most of the time hunting Little One's game. He liked to be alone when he was ready to prowl. At this time, he was going for a two to three day journey. He had become knowledgeable of the reeds' hidden and concealed spots. He met animals that were never seen by his brothers and Little One. As a matter of fact, he was many times able to meet with a human because he smelled the herdsman's campfire, and shepherd's thick sweat, from faraway. However, probably because of his distrust of the smoke, he made cautious and big detours. Aside from that, other big things never caused him to sidestep. He had a great assuredness and boldness; he did not know of any other being that he should get out of the way from. Perhaps by chance, one day Great Hunter became to know fear and helpless horror. More than a few days roaming and prowling amidst the reeds, with strength and a full belly; the summer gave an easy and soft plunder to the beast of prey.

Still, Great Hunter felt low-spirited himself, and this weakness was preying on his mind. It felt like he was tired; however, he had rested well at night. He also felt hungry despite having eaten some young birds at morning. His legs took him forward heavily and wearily. He had never felt this way before; he could not understand. Why? Great Hunter had no knowledge of cause-and-effect connections, and even if he had tried to explain his own strange condition, his thoughts went back to the encounter with the fox. The fox had a litter; and at the end of the reeds and in front of the fox hole, she played with them on the warm day. Great Hunter followed the smell. Around the fox hole it was full of bones, feathers, and rotten meat. These scents bothered his nose from faraway. Great Hunter watched the foxes play for a while even if the waiting game came hard to him. He held himself back, and with instinct, hatred rushed between them. The young foxes with a brisk move at once in the hole, like a mouse. The mother, to win some time for her litter to hide, turned on Great Hunter, with flashing teeth. The fox had calculated that the wolf-looking dog would stop for an instant, like all the other shepherd dogs before. In the meantime, she would be able to jump after her litter.

However, her calculation was wrong; it was all she could do in the last moment of her life. One sharp bite was taken. Great Hunter felt that the fox meat was smelly; it was not for eating, but out of curiosity, he tasted it. It really had a bad taste, and after he tore it up a little, he left the fox on the ground. Now he was feeling it; that's why he had that strange, feverish, sick, feeling. The Great Hunter became sick much later, in any case, if the soul and instinct became imbalanced, we could call it sickness.

At night he was sitting on the watch for a lookout. Big russet animals jumped in front of him at the cutout of the reeds. Similar to the fox—only much bigger— but, still smaller than Great Hunter.

He had never seen a wolf before, but still recognized them right away. He felt hate and attraction at once; he wanted to attack them and sometimes liked to run with the pack. His mother and father's blood struggled in him, and mixed feelings made him almost paralyzed. Possibly, the wolves smelled his scent, but did not care for him. If they met at winter, they most surely would start to fight. And even if Great Hunter could kill a few, he would pay with his life because there were many of them. However, at summer, the wolves took it easy and acted with cowardice. They did not like a toothed prey. And they disappeared and left the halfway-paralyzed cousin at his lookout post.

Great Hunter came back from his stupor and to his old self quickly. It was like forgetting the call, and a repulsive feeling for that wolf pack stirred inside of him. But somewhere inside of him, that feeling settled down and made him feel heavy, as though he had eaten too much. However, as we had said before; Great Hunter did not know for himself why this feeling had occurred, which is why he was suspicious of the fox. Inattentively and without any care he went out further and toward them; here, he did not need to watch out for the cunningly surfaced moor-swamp. The clear open waters were sparsely dappled with thin reeds. However, he was mostly traveling on solid ground. At once, he stopped so quickly like someone at the edge of a rift in the earth. One animal stood in front of him: a huge one. At top of his head, it wore sharp-pointed bones like a roebuck, except this animal was much bigger and his horns were more like branches; the mass of the body was much greater than the deer. Great Hunter never saw a stag before, but he felt standing in front of him power and domination. The stag looked at Great Hunter for a moment with unmoved eyes; Great Hunter's reckless instinct was telling him to attack the great deer.

Great Hunter dared to do so. Some weakness and fear came to him about the huge animal, which was bigger, and was going to win against him. Slowly and with ease, Great Hunter pulled back and crept away. From that incident, the stag came to his senses that one wolf would not scare him. But his experience told him that a pack of wolves could pull down even the strongest stag. The stag quickly jumped and with a clatter ran into the reeds. Great Hunter leapt once when the stag moved and then stopped to relax, simply listening as the great body clattered away. Great Hunter did not feel shame for his cowardly act because to an animal, it was not shameful to step out of the way of one who walked along the stronger path. Because the first law of the animals and often to humans as well was to stay alive! Sometimes one finds the will to stand up when they are commanded by extraordinary circumstances forced upon them, like a mother bird, fighting male animals, or a starved predator. A human's reflection deems these traits as courageous, and even with animals, it was considered courageous. Whomever this so called cowardice touched, and however the humans called out this cowardice, was found, in the most part, only in the animals that had been ruined by humans. Great Hunter went forward again, and felt no shame. Even though the encounter with the stag weakened him; he became insolent again and was cautious. He became like his old self. And he did not suspect for a moment after that fearful event that a bigger fright awaited him, the very same day.

It was already sundown when he passed underneath a big hollow willow tree. He stopped suddenly because he heard something stirring from the top of the tree. He was listening. Again, he heard noises stirring. He looked up towards the top of the tree, but was not able to see even a single bird. The noise persisted. Great Hunter pointed his nose upward to catch the scent of whatever was moving. He was definite from the smell he caught that this was a carnivorous bird. He walked around the tree and looked but could not see anything. The only evidence was a few disgorged balls of hair. However; balls of hair could not stir. Now that the rustle subsided; he stared fixedly and listened. After a little bit of time, he heard a scratching sound. His nose told him that all this noise came from the big tree. The low stir repeated itself again. The fire of a killer flared up in Great Hunter's eyes. Where the tree bifurcated, he saw a big hollow opening; now he knew by his nose that the unknown animal was in the hollow.

Great Hunter stood up on his two hind legs and with his front legs leaned on the tree trunk. He reached with precision into the opening of the hollow. He pushed his head into the hole. From the dark bottom of the hollow, two large yellow eyes stared fixedly and savagely at him. Something shouted at him, "Bu-hu", and a sharp object cut into his nose and small sharp needles grabbed and squeezed his eyes so hard that they filled up with tears. He was in a panic and tried to pull his head out of the hole but the needles did not let him go. On top of that, the unknown bird lashed his head with two wings around Great Hunter's eyes. The bird had a strong sharp beak and was giving out an ugly shout. Great Hunter almost became insane. He tried wriggling himself out, and his nose hurt even more. His claws slipped down from the tree trunk and filled with bark. Great Hunter fumed with fear as the great owl beat and hammered the intruder. Great Hunter roared. He felt his strength leaving him. With desperation, he threw himself backward and was able to pull the owl out from the hole. Outside, he let the owl loose and it flew away sluggishly. All the birds that were getting ready to rest for that night had a great hatred for the owl that attacked with a frightful scream. Great Hunter did not care for it and pulled his neck into his shoulder, and with an aching and bleeding nose, and rumbling head; he shambled away from the big willow tree. He so hated the owl clan, that he made a big roundabout when he sensed their smell. However, he was not called Great Hunter so that he would torment himself with fear. At night, he rested on the small island of reeds, and in the morning, with his luck, he was able to catch two young ducks. When he reached the hut, he was acting like someone who conquered the reeds. He ran Swimmer off from his usual bush. He beat Runner up just to show who was boss, and took his food. Basa escaped this wicked act only because she was on the hunt, and by the time she came home, Great Hunter was already sleeping under his willow bush.

CHAPTER 12

The form of an animal was probably structured by the same process as a human's was. However the inner changes we cannot prove. What we can see mostly is the exterior taking shape: teeth, bones, and muscles grow. To be skillful in self-defense, taking prey down, and gaining experience was developed through cunning. This trait of cunningness helps the animal catch prey as well. Precisely when a puppy grows up, we are able to recognize a great change and some exceptional things. Maybe the individual characteristics within the dogs' formation only welcome an immediate cause, or so we suspect. To write a description of the evolution of the dog, the ones written in novels about humans, would need to be measured up against a truth requirement and would still be difficult, and take a great deal of prowess. Perhaps, the difficulty comes because human beings did not develop the same way as the animals. Even if they did, we can only hear about the animals authentically when they start to write about themselves. This was the reason why the chronicler of this particular book only illustrated scenes about Basa and the puppies: the predacious life scenes. And if we were to take out of those scenes, the surrounding loosely connected scenes, the narrative development would probably unfold the same way because the characters—for the most part—are always partially growing. The scenes of this book were picked with a high hand.

It could have been possible to write some different variation of momentous occurrences. For instance, how the wolf father of Basa's litter returned and desired to eat his own puppies, how the angry Basa chased the wolf away, how Little One went to the human house to steal and got beat up with sticks, how Runner became sick from meat, how Basa was able to cure Runner with different types of medicinal herbs, and other adventures.

A chronicler needs to recognize the requirements of novel writing and be afraid of repetition---forced to leave those scarce scenes without mention. But rushing his pen with the intention of reaching the end of the scene, when even with human eyes, he is able to see great changes in the scene. For the above- mentioned reasons, the new upcoming changes could be shown as a series of pictures, such as is typical of characters not much different than before, but with content of entirely another kind.

The alert Great Hunter who slept under the bush sensed something was wrong. He held his nose high and a strong stinging smell hit his nose. He stood up, but by that time, he did not need to sniff with his nose because there was a torch light of fire in the night coming up in front of his eyes. The terror in the sounds of the reeds reached his ears. Contrary to his usual habits, he barked once because that redness was almost unknown to him. The smell was the same as the faraway campfire of the herdsman, but with those campfires the threat suggested was usually uncertain. But this time, there was undoubtedly danger to his life. Great Hunter was sure of himself as a grown dog, but would have liked it better if Basa took a look at the unknown threat that quickly approached.

He barked one more time. The brothers came out drowsy. The last to come was Basa who felt easy with the passing time. All of them became stiff; their nose up in the air sensing a flame storm from far away. Basa immediately became restless and with a low-voiced whining ran up and down the island. Her kids looked at her with dismay at her uncharacteristic behavior, and did not know what to think. No nearby prey showed itself, and that redness in the night was still faraway. Basa knew the fire well, and she felt it getting nearer. She ran to her kids, urging them gently with her nose one by one, and with her shoulder pushed them the other way. The kids growled back angry at her, resisting for they did not want to go. Basa gave up at last. She sat down and stared at the fire.

At the bottom of the sky darts of flames flew up high with black and red fire wings under them. A steam-covered giant black water buffalo bellowed with eyes like glowing embers and rushed headlong into the others, crushing and stamping their hooves on the reeds. The black ash flew like an invasion of locusts with an enormous hiss devouring the starry night. Covering what was left of life, sizzling and sucking the life out of everything, flying up again and floating to kill. The reeds were burning. The reeds' stems shot up like boiling water. The reeds' roots were bursting hot water geysers, shooting into the air. The small ponds were boiling; all the fish in it were cooked, and their bodies bobbed up and down in the boiling water until covered with the flight of ashes.

The reeds were screaming. Out of their sleep in the night, the beat-up birds were roused and slapped their wings in a stupor. The four-legged animals broke and crushed the reeds, fleeing away from the fire. They ran side by side: deer, wolves, hares, water snakes, big voles, and mice, crawling and running from reed to reed. The screeching sky was awake. The wind pushed the thick smoke forward; after the smoke, the rumbling fire came. The diminutive mouse nests burned down and what hung on the reeds, along with everything else; including the bird colony.

The weak and slow became the victims of the smoke---even a flying bird was caught by the high fire. The snakes' fine scaly skin burned, with sizzling frogs bursting up. The birds' black bones turned to dust and were covered with ashes; hares got charred lying on their sides--cramped as they still wanted to run. A roebuck with a broken leg, his antler licked around with red flames of fire, looked like a constellation of stars sparkling amidst the branches.

By this time, Basa's kids started to become restless. The fleeing animals passed by with great rumbling and they seemed not to care for the waiting dogs; one of the deer almost tipped Great Hunter over. The group of mixed animals waded across the small island, jumped into the water, and clamored into the reeds. The fire was burning very close, the whiff of heat made them uneasy. The thick smoke brought up by the wind, and spread over them like a big rag. The instinct of self-preservation told them that it was time to flee. Now they entrusted Basa entirely to lead them away. True! Basa knew the fire better than any animal in the reeds, but that knowledge would not be enough against the big fire. Her instinct ordered her to run where the big open waters were and where the reedless meadow grass was. The flight was a struggle of power; even a meat eater did not care for running side by side with a grass eater who would be prey at another time. The power now came in the senses as jostling, shouldering, trampling, overtaking, and passing.

Basa, with her four giant kids, ran over and through the reeds and water; on the writhing, crying bodies like a wild herd. Their furry hair was filled with reed-grass and leeches, and rush-shreds stuck into them; their legs hurt by the reed stumps that were covered by soft mud and duckweed. Behind their backs, the fire was raging. The glowing white heat, almost scorched their bodies. Above, wreathes of clouds of smoke choked the reeds, and all over the screaming cries of distress resounded, a sound more terrible than what a wild animal could not hear.

That is how they got through to the open waters and out to the grassy meadows where all the fleeing groups of animals stopped and scattered to find a hiding place to rest. At the big open water on the other side, the fire stopped and raged, unable to get farther; however, the wind helped to bring some sparks of fire along and burned the reeds up in the grassy field. Here and there, the fire burned the green grass. Very soon, the fire calmed down, the heat softened, the flames shriveled, and the smoke thinned away. The following night, the blowing wind stopped; the wildly bellowing pitch of the black buffalo could not be heard from the reeds.

By morning, the same places smoldered in the ravaged ground.

Intermittently, the flames shot up from the concealed glowing embers and the bluish willow' the wisps burned. The hot air still trembled above from the black destruction because the live coal from deep down pushed the heat, but the overall outbreak of fire had stopped. Farther on the other side of the open water, the ocean of reeds waved untouched with a new hiding place, inviting the fleeing animals. Some of them found a place in the rush at the fire's dwindling, but most of the animals scattered around the grassy field. Like some unwritten law ordering this never-seen-before giant encampment: they were able to live together as the danger hung above their heads. The meat eater rested next to the grass eater: deer, hares, were rarely frightened from wolf, fox, or snake. Here, on the meadow mostly four legged animals rested; the fast light winged birds disappeared into the unscathed parts of the reeds, except for a couple of herons and storks wo were preening their feathers on the meadow trees.

Until the upcoming morning that followed the fire, all the enemies lived in the house of the Garden of Eden. Although this was now the time and place for the practical Great Hunter to catch a hare. And the next moment, he jumped at the whole encampment with a grudge. Great Hunter started the everyday normal lifestyle, and nobody wanted to be left out. By the time Basa with the other three kids had come back from a successful hunt, the grassy field became deserted. Only Great Hunter sat on the hare and sometimes lifted up his blood-smeared nose. When all of them finished eating, they drank from a fresh, clear brook and went to look for a new lair in the reeds that was untouched by fire.

As always, Basa led the group with a slow trot; her grown-up kids were always behind her in a single Indian file. To the animals with a full stomach, they were never in a hurry. Basa and her family rested from time to time and went to hunt by evening. For a while, they just stayed at the edge of the reeds on the hard ground, looking at the wild animals' tracks and footprints at what the human eyes were not able to see. The evening hunt did not look like as successful of a hunt anymore. All the animals were on high alert here; even the smallest stir of a leaf made them jump and run away. These conditions are probably what brought a big change in the dogs' lives, or the chance that all of them were together in one spot, or it could have been that the aging Basa took it easy and slow, because she felt it getting harder to catch prey each time.

Little One noticed the doe-deer first who nipped on fresh, new grass. All at once, they started running toward the deer; but, Basa, who was getting tired from the hunt stopped at the edge of the reeds. Great Hunter! Great Hunter! Nobody saw him disappear; only he was not in the hunters' line up. Runner, Swimmer, Little One, dashed out from the reeds toward the doe-deer. She sensed and recognized the running dogs. She was fleeing. The three of them instinctively procured the prey.

Runner looked like he was swimming in the grass with a stretched-out body, the way he hurried forward to cut off the fleeing deer's ways. Behind the deer was the surprisingly agile Little One trotting; at her left-side behind and about thirty yards away was Swimmer pushing himself with a heavy but stubborn run. If the deer was healthy, only Runner would be able to match up to the doe-deer's speed. However, even he would not start alone with a big prey like that. Unfortunately for the deer, she was big and young but moved cumbersomely. Runner cut in front of her and drove in front of the other two hunters. The deer, with a daring cunning, tried to make up what she lost in speed because of pregnancy; when Runner was close to her, she spun around quickly and started to run toward Little One who stopped short. That big brown animal wanted to attack her; it was not her taste to fight with a thing like that. That would rather be a task for Great Hunter.

She jumped aside from the dashing deer. By the time Swimmer clumsily reached Little One, the deer was ahead with an advantageous lead; she was running with all her might toward the reeds, and if she could reach it, they most possibly would not catch her. And then there would be no dinner. So, the sound of the hunting dogs' chorus started in unison: Little One's deep huffing mixed with Runner's thin, piping voice, and Swimmer's rasping bark. For a while, Little One held her own, drawing behind the fleeing deer because she was never afraid of whatever ran away from her, and now she tried to make up for her last "bravado"---what we can call cowardice on the same page. Runner overtook Little One very soon and passed by like a flying hawk; Runner again was the closest to the deer. However, the deer's advances were too much even for the great Runner, so she would be able to reach the safety of the reeds. The deer knew that too, and the last yards she ran with full power. Basa waited for the scene to end from the cover of the reeds' edge. When the deer broke away from Little One, Basa was under the protection of the high standing reeds; she slunk to where the deer was running. However, she did not count on the small brook to turn away the deer from her path. Because of that, she was unable to jump; she had to run forward to be able to stop the fleeing deer.

The deer could not stop and did not even turn away; in front of her stood a huge white dog. In her fear of death, she jumped high, and taking into account her heavy weight, would be a rare thing to do. The deer flew over the dog's head and with her hind legs hoof grazed the dog's furry back. Basa was counting on the deer to stop and then planned to jump on her. But, to her surprise, her opened-up jaw used for biting, closed—it was more for protection than to catch the prey. Basa turned around quickly and saw the deer's white haunches reflect like a mirror between the swaying reed sticks. There ran the dinner, unmatched. At that moment, she unexpectedly saw a big gray body flying toward the deer. The deer cried and fell down. Great Hunter's whole body lay on the back of the deer, holding her throat. He had been following the hunt and hurried to get in front of the deer like his mother.

That short period of time that Basa held back the deer was enough time for Great Hunter to cut off the deer's escape. Great Hunter heard Basa's teeth clattering, and he knew his mother had missed the prey. The deer ran only a few yards away from him. To Great Hunter's relaxed muscles, it was child's play to reach the already-tired, overdriven beast. By the time the others reached the kill, the deer's big dark eyes had grown dim. Basa and her kids growled together with envy; one snarled at the other and flashed their teeth, tearing up a collectively caught prey.

By chance, that collective hunt was a repeat of the memorably puppy-hood hare hunt when Great Hunter got beat up by his brothers at the end. However, that first collective hunt was a repeat in and of itself: the repeat of the ancestors' hunt because the life of the animal always repeated itself through its parents' ways. The animal repeated the life of its parents, and they breed. Still, what made and formed Basa and her kids as a team was an unusual situation. They came from singularly hunting individuals into a powerful team. The team was not an occasional alliance like hunting stray dogs who, two or three of them, coming together to catch and bring down a hare and then break up and scatter away afterward. Basa's team was similar to the wolf's more permanent pack. The ancient way of life forced them to live out a lifestyle of ancient manners of living. They killed two lives with the pregnant doe-deer, and that success taught them about the benefits of a collective hunt.

Since then, it became very rare for them to hunt alone, only for birds and fish because those animals cannot be hunted collectively. Hunting with a pack was more successful. And that success came bundled with the ecstasy of freely open sounding throats, chasing horrified victims of prey.

To Basa's or Great Hunter's fangs, that was worth everything. The plan they formulated as a pack became a formula. It did not matter what the selected victim was; hare or deer. They enacted the same formula all the time, and they became more skillful and cunning every time. With Runner's leadership, Little One's and Swimmer's pursuit and procurement of the game, where Basa waited with ease or where the perfect killer Great Hunter hid; even Basa would not lose out and miss her prey, clanking her teeth emptily like before. The selfish Great Hunter now could not appropriate the prey for himself even if he was the one who pulled the prey down, because the four of them stood against him. And even Great Hunter's boldness got the message on how far he could go.

Until now, Basa's puppies were dangerous, predacious beasts, but now they became tame lives most fearful of ravaging. And they were so successful that it became depopulated around their new den very soon. Even those left alive like hares, deer, and water birds, moved away. But the smaller rapacious animals, like fox, weasels, and others had to look for a new lair. At their new place, they did not hunt around their lair. They went far away for prey. Out of Basa's cleverness they picked the resting place that was protected by water and swamp; it was a hard-to-reach, soft, tricky surface here, and they could not hunt as a pack for there was a grass land and a firm ground covered with scanty reeds growing out of the firm ground. The lair could only be reached with difficulty, through the narrow marshy bog, or swimming by water. The five dogs were able to hide in their fortification.

The time arrived when Basa's instinct could save her kids' lives; the way she picked the new lair was clever, if the extremely cold winter did not interfere and freeze all the waters in the reeds. We should be talking about the "band" hunting. Probably we would not need to say that they had bad hunting days more often when the wide-awake game jumped up. During those times, the hunters went to sleep hungry. The unsuccessful activity occurred in the same manner as the successful ones, except the outcome was different. The uniformity characterized what we call "band" hunting. If the chronicler was able to find some outstanding difference of the two kinds of hunts, he would write it down if it were worth something. And the end, he was unable to do so. However, our heroes killed their victims at the end most of the time.

From this narrative's point of view, the dogs were heroes: all five of them, in so much as for the story is sympathetic toward its principal figures. However, according to the poor aesthetic tastes of the reeds' animals of prey and their point of view, the killers were predatory and merciless. We should not say that either of the views was true. The predator, if the balance is equal between species, is not predatory but a necessary and natural occurrence. In saying so, they are neither good nor bad: the arbitrary human rules could deem the hunting activities cruel and immoral, for instance, the pregnant doe-deer pull down. But in the world of the reeds, it was not cruel and immoral, but natural—like a bird hunting for bugs. Since this is a written book, no matter how much we strive to show the real life appearance relayed with an amount of certitude, stories are still not real life. Basa and her puppies should remain heroes and lovely, because this bias story is specifically written about them.

Two of our heroes' hunting lives should be told, even if the hunting uniformity was no different from the others; still, the size and power of their game distinguished them from the other hunters. The first event was defeating the stag. The stag, not the one whom Great Hunter became scared of previously, came from some faraway forest and into the reed country. Maybe hunters chased it out from the ready-for-fall forest, were the stags start belling and bulls fight for a mate, a partner, underneath the rusty leaves, shaking bushes, or openings of the rough grass field. Perhaps, it was the wolves or dogs chasing them away.

Nobody knew---only the stag knew---why it turned up in this stinking, muddy, entirely different, not fitting world. But, on his side, showed blood clots and wounds. He obviously was not walking through the reeds' cold waters for the fun of it. He had great-sized branching antlers; we can call them eighteen-point antlers. Little One caught a glimpse of him. For a long time, she looked at the curious animal from the reeds with respect, which, with suspicion— lifted his head up from the small brook. Little One was out on her usual voluntary spying adventures, and not because she was so ardent but because of some unreasonable desire's command. With a silent move, she pulled back. If she wanted, she could walk into the rattling reeds, like a white phantom dog. Her brothers, with Great Hunter in the lead, went to scrounge. Little One had to run for a while until she caught up with them. She could not speak, but Great Hunter figured out that she was talking about big game, from the way she was acting. With a hunting trot, all of them closely followed Little One.

The stag disappeared from the grassy field. After running around a couple of laps, Little One tracked the stag's scent. Now, Runner led the pack; not because he was the best tracker, but nobody would be able to hold him back. It was not hard to follow the stag's trail; his strong smell was sensed from afar; his hooves left deep marks in the soft soil.

For a while, the stag slowly trudged on to the grassy meadow, then cut into the thing edge of the reeds and walked farther in. It was easy to read his track marks here. The stag had stopped biting the grass, and the four hooves left a deeper mark to the left of the track, and the size of his palm spotted the mangled grass and left it standing up. Here, he jumped once; the hind hooves cut deep, and from the reed stalk trickled down the memory of the slimy spring flood. The rush leaves broke down as the big body turned with a sudden move. Great Hunter scanted around. That made the big bull jump not far off from the track. His nose got a light scent of the wolves. The hair around his neck stood up.

The wolves no doubt came around at night. The bull walked rather at random, rattling out of the thin reeds and resumed his walk. The trail became wide and deep: the bull was running. All five dogs ran stretched-out, going after the stag. At once, out of Runner's throat, a raspy short bark broke out. There in front of them rambled the antlered creature, angrily butting his head here and there into a gray-green willow bush. He became irritated from the smell of wolves, and, now in his humiliation tested his power on the bushes by imitating a fight and enraging himself. The five dogs started off at a running speed. Basa and Great Hunter instantly pushed toward the reeds. Runner, with a half circle, tried to cut off the bull's retreat behind them. Swimmer trotted with the philosopher, Little One, as she looked at the situation objectively. It was better if she slowed down and stayed behind Swimmer, because the bull's ceremony cooled down her enthusiasm. Runner flew through, and above bushes and puddles. Parallel to him— at the reeds' edge, was Great Hunter running, not as spectacular and graceful—but almost at the same speed.

Runner neared the stag with his head held high and started to run toward it. And now the hunting dogs' sounds broke out into different choruses. "The prey is fleeing. We are after blood and meat in our empty stomach. Quickly running on four legs, our strong white fangs, and the beating heart of the hunt. We are after him! Jump at him! Jump at his throat, pull down this runaway. Slow down his run, stumble him.

Stop! You coward, stand still, wait for us and fight. After him! After his blood and meat, for our eager red throats."

And the bull stopped. Maybe his irritation made him stop and become tired of the chase and the agony of fear. Perhaps, he was not afraid of the dogs, because he did not suspect a human behind them. He stopped and held his antlers in the attack position. Runner, who was the closest to the stag, suddenly slowed down and was surprised by the bull's behavior. He probably would jump on him from behind, but became afraid to attack up front against the many-forked weapons the stag bared. In his helplessness, he sat down and barked at the bull. To stop Swimmer was impossible once he started. He rushed by his brother and jumped at the bull. The attack almost cost Swimmer his life. The bull slashed with his giant antler in an upward direction. If that movement had reached Swimmer under his belly, he probably would have hardly hunted again on the collective hunts. Luckily, the antler only reached his side and slashed it up; Swimmer turned himself over and heavily thumped on the ground. The bull dashed forward to finish Swimmer when Little One bit into the bull's hind leg. For that she got a big kick, and with a loud cry flattened out in the grass. Somehow, Swimmer was able to stand back up and with his stubborn style, attacked again. Now, both of them missed the mark. It was probable that Swimmer's fear of the antlers held his jump short, and the bull's slash missed him. Great Hunter watched the game with his instinct; Runner's helpless bark notified him of the trouble. Great Hunter stopped! He looked at the ruckus and saw when Swimmer fell to the ground. Great Hunter started running toward the bull.

When the bull noticed a new enemy, it quickly turned to face him and waited. However, Great Hunter did not get his name to just run into the antlers senselessly, as Swimmer did. With a quick-curving glide in front of the running bull, he nipped into the bull's front leg and tried to get under the beast's belly. The bull was an expert warrior and had knowledge and finesse. He jumped high and started to run faster. He felt that the position gave him a disadvantage and tried to scatter his enemies. At the edge of the reeds, Basa waited for him. The bull's dash was against her; Basa jumped aside, and at her second jump, grabbed into the bull's shiny black nose. The bull shuddered and clattered along. Basa let herself chase the stag for a while, when Runner and Runner came too close and turned into them.

There, the stag twirled, slashed, attacked, and defended himself from the barking; and the attacking dogs were so agile and as skillful as a cat. It was amazing how lightly the dogs' big bodies moved; they sometimes sat down, helplessly licking their wounds and looking at each other steadily in the eyes. It was all about the victim who was now being driven to the walls. The sides of them were dented, shaking from the forced exertion. The bull's breast was also heaving at its sides, and blood flowed from its legs, caused by the deep bites at his large red and meaty breast; which showed that Basa still had not lost her power. Her hair was soaked, black with blood. They were looking at each other: the heaving stag and the heaving dogs. The dogs knew that the prey would belong to them sooner or later. And the stag knew that he could not take it much longer. They were resting their muscles, shaking it off— ready to start again.

The stag quickly dashed at Great Hunter, and the wolf dog saw it was better to jump aside. And, again, the bull started to run. They were getting deep into the reeds; the bull with shooting dark red eyes, and a beating pulse did not look where he was running anymore; just taking flight.

He stopped again, fought back, and ran again. At once his knees buckled. He tried to pull them up, but the other leg sank deeply downward. A wild, terrible feeling ran through him; he tossed and turned and tried to pull his legs up, but they sank deeper. With lighter bodies and knowledge of the swamp, the dogs leapt back to the dry ground when they felt the shaking underneath their paws; the deceptive surface of the velvety ground. And from there, they looked at the big bull's struggling agony. The bull sank deeper and deeper. At first only his four legs disappeared; his body swayed above the surface like a branching tree-trunk without limbs, like an ancient idol. Trembling with tiredness, his great-looking head often tumbled down toward the deceptive silky grasses surface, but with enormous effort lifted his head up as the crown of his antlers hit the back of his behind. The stag's wide stomach held him up above the surface; only his legs struggled down in the leachy deep black mud. And then, they disappeared entirely. The deep swamp pulled him down. After a little time, only the sorrowful head and antlers was above the bubbling water, making round circle waves running up and outward to cover the silky grass. Basa was sitting with her kids around the stag's grave, and they looked at it with agitation. Their sorrows dejected as the lot of meat vanished. When the mount of antlers sank underneath the waters' surface; all of them started to let out a wild, sad cry.

The other big game of the two hunts mentioned was a more fortunate venture than the stag. Even if they were unable to become victorious over the wild boar, the measure of the hunt was not in counting the wounds and was not even in their level of bravery, but the potential satisfaction of a full stomach.

Similar to the big bull's death, many other troubles would pile onto the cold winter, following the light and easy fall, filled with sunlight. An early freeze arrived without snow, taking away the cold freeze's sharp edge. The dogs' claws were hurting from the hard ground, and a needle-sharp reed thread became stuck into the numb paw pads, and there a painful wound became poisoned and infected. The wild game available was less than usual during wintertime. Even from the north, migrating birds flew away. Those who stayed home died off, or disappeared, and a beast of prey with a lean body and disheveled fur dragged itself in to the world of the reeds.

At other times, Great Hunter always found some food for himself with the pros of his egoism and skillfulness; now hungry and with irritation, he staggered like the others. They fought every day, and that did not stop with common sense but weakness and hunger; Basa bickered with her kids, and the kids bickered with their mother and between themselves; they were exhausted afterward and stretched out on the icy hard ground. Only Little One stayed away from the quarrels; she felt, the command is the law of the wolf's heirs, who became seriously wounded, ripping prey into parts and taking food from each other. The truth was, the dogs did not have enough strength to impart a real, serious wound, even if they gathered around the fighters or even until they got into a fight amongst themselves and waited in vain for the signs of gushing blood. The light, easy bites left a reddish trace on fur. That was called the great famine. Even Basa had no memories of such a frozen state as this. They stood watching as the bones of the earth broke through the surface of the wintery ground. Basa's own self—in her timidity— remembered her life under the protection of humans. Finally the snow fell down, but that brought more trouble: so deep was the snow that they all needed to swim on their stomachs to transport themselves. Still, that snow helped them; after fighting with a wild boar, they were able to eat some warm meat and get back their strength. The wild boars came around the reeds, even if it did not happen often, it happened more frequently than a stag's arrival. Until then, they were afraid to attack the angry animal. They would not have attacked had the winter not been so hard and the hunger so commanding. The big sow bore itself into the snow at the bottom of the reeds' bog. Four of her piglets lay around their mother. They were weak and lean, leaner than the usual wild boars during wintertime. The cold winter ate away the fat that they put on before the snowfall. Now, the thick deep snow hid the food from them, and the skin stuck into their ribs. The wild boars sometimes slept deeply and carelessly: they did not even awake when Basa and her kids came around them.

However, if they came with a wind, they could give the dogs a disadvantage. That is what occurred to Swimmer when he almost stumbled over the black bristled back of the boar that bulged out of the white snow. He growled, and the others dashed over there. By that time, the sow was up and, with her small and vicious eyes, measured them up. The wild boars usually walked away if small dogs attacked them and would only sometimes turn around on them. But she had an anger toward the big dogs who were willing to fight with her. Here she was, a sow protecting her piglets. She quickly turned; the crystal snow splashing all over and throwing back the attacking dogs. Those who got thrown into the snow were lucky; some of them got bitten. Runner was the only one who was able to jump away unhurt.

However, their hunger took away their thinking powers and they attacked the angry black devil again from up front. Everything happened the same way as how they would attack during the summertime: only their movements were slower. Both the boar and the dogs' legs were shaking, lungs gasping for air and becoming short winded. The attackers could not care that the deep snow hindered their own feeble fighting. In a way, their character grew used to it. The dogs had some advantage with long legs, but that advantage against the angry sow only helped at times of flight, but not when they attacked. The stubborn animal did not even notice the light bites that could not pull her down, and getting close to the more vital parts was impossible.

Until the fight went on; the four piglets scattered in the snow, and from afar, they were looking back. Only one piglet ran franticly until it got stuck in the deep, unbroken snow. At the end, the piglets and Little One stopped the fight in the tiring snow. Little One soon realized that the sow was too strong and dangerous; besides, she started chasing one of the young piglets. She quickly grabbed it; the little piglet's short legs could not compete with Little One's long legs. When the mother sow heard a squeal, she threw off the attackers with a blow and dashed to save her piglet. At that moment on the other side, a scream of a piglet broke out. Basa recognized here that the only way to win was through the execution of Little One's method. The boar's mother turned toward Basa, but she did not wait for the angry sow who could not reach Basa in time. Farther away, a piglet got stuck and screamed between Great Hunter's jaws. For Great Hunter, a fifty-yard advantage was enough to finish his work. By the time the mother boar reached the spot where Great Hunter grabbed the piglet, she could only see a gray back vanish into the reeds, and the piglet was nowhere to be seen. Now the others, like they were playing a game, did the killing act. It was not a thought that made them play the killer game, but the instinct of a common sense appropriateness---often strikingly similar to a thought. The piglets were in a helpless situation; they were too close to the dogs. They were the ones who were an easy prey, and a beast of prey did not want to fight but to eat. Actually, that was what led Basa into action.

We said that Basa recognized the advantage of Little One's method. However, that assumption was not illegitimate due to the fact that she lived with a human for several years. By the time the mother sow came back, two of the dogs had pulled down one piglet and killed it with Basa's pulling bites. The three dogs jumped on the two other piglets. The piglets tried to stumble back to their mother; but the dogs did not let them, pulling and grabbing at them. At other times, they were agile and quick, but in the deep snow, they were heavy moving little black animals. And the boar, in her angry motherly trod, went between the dogs and her piglet; however, the quick dogs jumped away and went for her other piglet. Finally, the mother sow realized the only possible route to protect her piglets. She called to the newly freed piglet and started out toward the other one. She could not go fast, because the little piglet became exhausted; by the time the mother reached the second one, it was already lifeless; hanging out of Swimmer's mouth. The sow became enraged and went after Swimmer. The advantage Swimmer had was because of his long legs; however, he lost that advantage, because the weight of the heavy prey in his mouth was slowing him down.

The angry, steam-blowing mother got very close, with Runner's constant bites having no effect on her. Swimmer felt that danger was close by, but not in any way would he give up his prey or let it go. Breaking the snow in front of him with a high-standing reed, the mother pig was only a few yards behind Swimmer who jealously guarded his prey and not himself. He was stubborn even at the very last moment, with muscles tightened, pulled, and he lifted the heavy young pig onto the snow and moved forward.

Little One played a helping role and saved the day, not because of her cleverness, but her cowardice and greediness. When the mother sow went after Swimmer and her piglet, Little One used her cunningness and pulled herself to the side; she was not in the mood to attack the mother as Runner did. Besides, the mother would be sorry to leave the only piglet who was left behind and who failed to come with a raging mother. So, Little One chased the piglet; at the loud screaming, the mother sow turned again because the living piglet was more important to her than the dead one. She turned back one last time because Basa's kids had no more strength left to fight with a frantic mother sow. Little One let go of the hard pressed piglet; Swimmer and Runner, with shaking legs and wet and dirty hair, vanished into the reeds.

The bloody and tedious occurrence of this hunt probably should have been enough. However, compared to the passing years, it was a small amount. But it was a carefully selected story that has been written down. It could be enough, if their prey hunts would mean a development and view of life suitable for their world. After all, we cannot live out the last but most important prey-hunt- related story but if only through these words. We would not know if the events crafted within this selection of words was an account or even reality about how to lead Basa's kids down the final road ahead. If until now, we saw the quickly passing years, the summaries and omissions we jumped through. The last parts are comparatively more faithful, following the reality of time and fact---because this synopsis only encompassed a few weeks. We are not going to reach the end of the winter that brought the great famine until we finish the tale. The extremely cold winter has thickened all events for us.

CHAPTER 13

SHEEP-WOLVES

Great Hunter led the pack. It was an unknown countryside to them; here, there were less reeds and the water became ice underneath the snow and at the faraway foggy, grey, horizon was a great stretch of flat land. He stopped suddenly and stretched his head forward. Usually, when he stiffened like a hunting dog, a hare lay flat in front of him or a bird had looked him in the eyes. The others were scantily smelling the air. A scent of smoke hit their noses, and this stopped Great Hunter. The morning dimness just cleared up. A radiant, strong, winter sun drew an unlikely misshaped shadow on the bluish snow. They were standing, bewildered. Then, Basa, who just remembered a long time ago when she committed the act of stealing sheep, took the lead and once more—for the last time—led her grown-up puppies. They were hungry and she knew where there was smoke there were sheep to find. The great hunger wiped the fright of man away; that is what drove the wolves to the houses, creeping against the wind.

Now, they could not go and jump on the prey with loud shouts; they must be cunning like a fox, or like their father—the wolf—when they were about to attack the flock of sheep. Shepherds were lolling around in the warmly heated reed hut. The dogs outside started barking abruptly. "Go outside and take a look at what is bothering them," the head shepherd told the youngest shepherd. He covered himself with sheepskin and went out. Basa and her kids were already fighting with the shepherd dogs outside. The sheep could not be seen from the reed fence, a wall; but their agitated movements revealed that the predators were breaking into the sheep flock. At the side of the stack of straw that fed the sheep during winter, Great Hunter was killing a black puli dog. The puli was already mauled, and tried to flee from the much bigger, wilder, and stronger dog.

The others were fighting with shepherd dogs, hard and victorious; however, Great Hunter raged with anger. In his wolf blood, the hatred for dogs came to surface; the pulis felt it and with high pitched screams ran away from him. Only Basa could not be spotted anywhere; she already broke into the sheep pen and tried to strangle a piebald lamb in the middle of the simple and defenseless flock. She was able to finish the sheep off much more easily four years ago. Quite a few times, she needed to jump. A few times, the sheep got loose from her jaws until she was able to bring it down again. And even after that, it took a while. By the time she closed her tired jaw on the victims throat; the shepherd boy looked at them for a moment, froze up, and screamed, "Wolves!" And with his shepherds crook, he ran menacingly toward Great Hunter who almost finished off the young puli.

Great Hunter lost his mind once he saw the boy nearing. For the last time, he bit into the dog, and he charged at the young shepherd. The boy became scared when he saw a giant wolf running at him. He blindly and instinctively struck with a big stick; however, he missed, turned around, and started running towards the hut. Great Hunter was astonished by the whistling stick flying in front of his nose; he would have stopped, but he could not resist the runaway, and chased after the young shepherd boy.

Suddenly, and with a loud chant, the shepherds swung their sticks and ran toward the intruders. Now this was too much, even for Great Hunter; he turned around, his tail between his legs, and took flight. All the others were running with him. On their tail were yelping dogs that became brave again after seeing their owners, but it was still more with sound than with bite. They pursued Basa and her kids.

The head shepherd stopped at the reed fence and looked into the flock. "Where was the piebald lamb?" he asked with an accusing tone; it was like the shepherds had taken it. They were coming around to see that the lamb was really missing. Farther on, where the sheep and the man did not tread; a trail of the lamb that had been carried away by the intruders was found in the snow. "Go after them," said the senior shepherd. "What was that? Wolves?" Confused, the sheepherder did not know what to say. Finally one of the others told him, "It was dogs."

"What dogs? Who is the sheepherder to whom the dogs belonged?" he asked them.

The sheepherders shrugged their shoulders. They knew all the dogs in the region, but they had not seen those in particular. Because those dogs had not been established by the head shepherd himself, he recognized that it was about five years at wintertime when the white wolf came around.

"The king wolf; I saw it that time. I was a senior shepherd throwing my stick. The next day I slipped on the ice and broke my leg. To the other sheepherders, that was a clear moral lesson of the story. "That was a king wolf with kids," continued the shepherd. "It was an evil shaman who was a wolf, but this time it came with a dog face. If we go after it, we would bring upon us a magic spell." They probably could catch up with Basa and her heavy prey, but because of the sheep herders hesitation, they were able to carry the lamb for a good while; when Basa met with Swimmer, together they carried it easily to their living area in the reeds—where the others were already waiting. The lamb quickly disappeared, devoured between the five dogs. They needed to look for new prey, but now they had found meat, lots of it: a big sheep flock and a herd of swine. They were not the easiest prey to catch, because they had to fight with dogs—not only with weak pulis, but with very strong komondors like themselves; however, the humans did not chase them away. They only stepped out of their hut and started to shout, but they never attacked the four legged devils.

Basa and her company did not have any idea why, or better yet they had no idea what kind of unearthly power protected their safety. They did not always visit the same sheep flock; they paid a visit to another sheep herder, not only for sheep but even swine herds. The swine herds were not safe anymore from Basa's band. It was a much harder job with pigs that with the simpleton sheep. However, the other sheepherders and swine herders would not bother them either; they only cursed at them in a godless manner.

In the reeds, the news went around quickly, especially if the wicked bringing trouble had the face of an animal. Many of the sheep herders remembered the ominous breaking of a leg a few years back. Basa and her band ravaged the neighborhood in peace. They never killed just for a kill, unlike the wolf that fell into the sheep flock and killed one after the other. Great Hunter could probably have had that inclination, but the band's habitude did not leave him free to start. Basa, and the misfortune of the hard winter, not only drove them towards the sheep but towards the wolf too. One day, Basa and her band met after a third or fourth predatory act. They were going home, pulling the sheep they killed. Mouths were steaming in the cold. Not long ago the legs of the sheep were agile, now the frozen stiffness already snuck up on their bodies. Not far from home, in the labyrinth of the reeds, the band of dogs legs were sliced by the sharp reeds; the paws were hurt by the hard crusted snow.

Then Swimmer noticed the wolves sniffing around their dens, who easily walked on the frozen ice that was not hard to get near, because of the frozenness. The wolves, eight of them, were fully grown strong animals. The breed in the reeds had reddish hair, and they were smaller in size than their grey cousin which hailed from the forest. However, they were as great in cunning and ferocity. The wolves had better eyesight than the dogs' weak sight. The wolves also noticed a nearing band, even if the band had the wind against them.

They started with a slow trot toward Basa and her band, on their bellies frozen snow and hanging ice had accumulated. Their stomachs were dented from hunger. They noticed the dead sheep almost immediately; now aside from their natural hatred, the envy of the prey now stirred inside of them. Inside of Basa, fear and hatred reverberated: the dog's fear and hatred against the wolf. That little attraction that Basa had years ago towards her kids' father now could not be re-lived or flared up from within her: now, she was against the wolf. Since olden times, there had been a war between the wolves and her breed. And, she was a descendent of the great herding dogs, and she felt it in every piece of her body. However, it was not her who led the band against the wolves; Great Hunter had much less shepherd-dog memory in his blood than any of them; every cell in his body was more wolf than dog. Great Hunter fought with prey in wolf style.

The five dogs pulled back to the wall of the reed fence so their backs would be safe from the attack behind them. They stood around the prey and waited. The wolves were attacking with snarls: all together, because wolves did not like to fight alone. Two hungry-looking older female wolves jumped at Swimmer. They were looking for his throat, but Swimmer held his head down and grabbed one of his attacker's nose and closed his jaw on it: bones were cracking. Swimmer was stronger. The wolf's legs stiffened up and try to free his badly injured nose from Swimmer's jaws, but Swimmer was as stubborn as a bulldog and did not let the wolf free. With his powerful body mass, he was able to move the wolf off balance, and in the meantime, his jaw was squeezing the bones. The other wolf bit Swimmer from the back, and with lucky bites broke Swimmer's hind leg. Out of pain, he squeezed his teeth, and when he opened his mouth, the wolf with the broken nose fled to the reeds. Swimmer turned to the wolf who had attacked him from behind, but the wolf who was more agile than the heavy moving dog, jumped away. The heavy-moving dog's movements were even heavier due to his injury. The wolf tried getting at Swimmer's throat in different places. Swimmer just turned with the wolf; his head was down and he looked for an opening, a chance to close his teeth on the wolf.

On Runner's back were two wolves. However, if the wolves were quick, Runner was quicker; looking from a distance, somebody would believe that the two wolves and the dog produced some play clowning—a friendly dance. Only the dancers' wounds showed that they were not in a play-mood. Rather, the high spirit of that quickness and the strengthening of muscles showed they were ready for a life and death fight. Runner bled from many wounds from the wolves, but his bones were untouched. None of them were able to make a deadly grab yet.

The wolves made their first mistake when they let Great Hunter fight with a male wolf alone. Great Hunter normally belonged to the wolves. Great Hunter's customs of fighting off wolves was more varied, accommodating his mixed dog instinct. Great Hunter, with his huge body, weight and power was more effective. At first, just like the style of the wolves—he grabbed for the throat. And, with a sudden change of tactics, he grabbed a wolf by the back of the head. The wolf bit into Great Hunter's chest, and blood started flowing down his front legs. Great Hunter leaned down and pushed the wolf who tried to escape from sure death. But this endeavor did not help to deviate the natural fate of the wolf. Great Hunter pushed and pinned the wolf down to the ground; when the wolf lost his balance, Great Hunter, with lightning speed, grabbed the wolf's throat. With that movement, the fight was over. The wolf was stretched out on the snow with an open throat. Great Hunter looked around. The wound on his chest did not take away his fighting spirit, it made his fighting mood more spirited than ever. Swimmer, who was closest in distance to Great Hunter, was whirling around in front of him. Great Hunter bided his time and waited for the best opportunity to jump at his attacker and pull it down from its feet. Swimmer limped to him and bit into the lying wolf's neck and angrily growled at Great Hunter as a sign to leave him alone with his prey.

Great Hunter let Swimmer have his way with his prey. From Swimmer's jaws, it would be hard to escape. Little One bellowed like a lion as she struggled with the wolf. The way Great Hunter saw it, it was better if he stepped into the dancer's show. And with Runner, the both of them quickly made the wolves run. In the meantime, Basa fought without sound. She felt that it was her last fight. She was not agile enough to fight off two opponents. She pushed half of her body into the reeds for better protection. One of the wolves clutched Basa. She grabbed the wolf's head and pushed it down as Great Hunter would; and with her full body weight closed her teeth and lied down on the wolf without movement. The pinned-down wolf thrashed up and down under Basa. All the while, the other wolf got closer to Basa's throat. Basa did not care. She was tired and just continued to lay on the beaten down wolf. Her teeth went deeper and deeper into its vertebral column. By the time she was able to reach it, the other wolf successfully reached her throat. Basa stretched out with a cramped jaw. The victim under her tried to kick her off, but Basa's cramped jaw did not allow it. Slowly the wolf calmed down. Runner and Great Hunter strangled Little One's opponent. They almost tore the wolf up alive. The wolf's entire body was an open wound, but he still snapped after Little One until Runner killed the wolf with a quick bite. Swimmer was still sitting on his killed wolf, with a wild growl—he tore it.

The other of Basa's opponents—the one who stayed alive—felt it better to run. It grabbed

the sheep, but Runner noticed; and the three of them ran after the thief. And the kids saw that their mother, Basa, lay stiff on her last prey. They went to her sniffling, and the most affectionate Little One sadly started to howl. The other two sniffled around for a while and then started pulling the sheep home. Four wolves lay on the battlefield, and Basa, Fodor Balazs serf-man's former dog. Basa's hair was not as white as the surrounding snow, but out of the cloudy sky; snowflake stars snowed softly down and covered Basa's fur with their own whitish color. Little One was hungry and soon went after the pulled sheep's tracks.

CHAPTER 14

THE HERDSMEN

After Basa's death, only three of the dogs were going after the sheep flocks, because Swimmer had a broken leg and could not go with them; remaining at his brothers' mercy.

Even in his sick bed, Swimmer had a great appetite; and because of that, his family had to fight with the sheepherders' dogs every second day. On one occasion, a wild sheepherder's boy who was a newly employed bastard, blustering the hut attacked Runner; saying he was not afraid of white wolves. Great Hunter and Little One hurried to Runner's aid and mauled the little boy badly. That was probably the last straw that provoked the herdsmen to end their patience on the toll Great Hunter and his band took. After they extorted another sheep, all the herdsmen and a head shepherd came together in the broken legged sheepherder's hut. Only one man and the dogs stayed to watch the sheep flocks. In the hut, the reed fire was crackling and the thick smell of lard circulated around the meat cooking in the stew pot; the men were sitting close together, barely able to move.

At present time, they reconciled the swine herder with the sheepherder; and from a distance, the horse herder and the cowboys were not engaging in rivalry on who ranked in first place. Spoons made from wood and bones plunged deep into the food; nobody said a word and they ate, chewing their meat noisily. Finally, the sheepherder who belonged to this place pushed the stew pot away and put some reed on the fire. The men took off their shirts, and sat naked down to the waist. One of the old head-shepherds who came from a faraway region listened to them tell the story about the white wolves. In the corner of the hut, sat the sheepherder's boy who had gotten mauled, and he showed his wounds. The old head-shepherd, who had a reputation as a shaman took a look at the wounds when they finished the story. He thought for a while. Nobody said a word. They sat motionless.

"Does anybody know where there resting place is?" asked the shaman man finally.

"Who would know?" asked the one who gave hospitality.

It was not a good omen to cross the shaman's path with even a little indiscretion, but the shaman did not pay attention to it.

"Nobody knows?"

"I know," said one of the sheepherder's who sat in the corner.

"They were at the outside glade."

The man of the reeds found his way in the mazes, because every part of the territory had a name.

The men knew that the outside glade was between the fox-reed and carcass pit corner, known by the grass fields people. Origins of the names were fading away; only the old, old sheepherder's bones would be able to explain their exact meaning. Because the fox-reed was uninhabited by foxes, and was covered entirely with water; and the carcass corner was an impenetrable, endless thick wall of reeds. The men did not care with names; they saw the land with the coming migration where the company of brigands dwell.

"At what time will they come?" asked the shaman man.

"At morning time. Tomorrow midday we will catch on to them. Every man must bring a good stick."

But the shaman interrupted the host. The shaman of the shepherds looked at him.

"I will take away their power," he said.

The four dogs were full, curled up, and lying down; only Swimmer stood up sometimes to try out his legs. He was able to run again. He stopped and growled. The others jumped up right away. It did not take much sniffing; their noses were struck with the scent of man. A lot of man smell. They were here, breaking the reeds and crackling the snow. Great Hunter quickly started to head toward the opposite side of the glade, and stopped suddenly. In front of him were the men breaking the dry reed.

At first the family of dogs tried to break out on one side and then on the other side. However, the men came, nearing in from everywhere. Now the fear snuck into their heart. They dispersed, and everybody looked for their own escape route. Swimmer became the first victim. When he realized that with his injured leg he would be unable to escape, he turned to his pursuer with snarling teeth. Despite his attempt to fend the men off, heavy sticks fell on him; and Swimmer's lifeless body stretched out in the snow. Runner played a trick on the sheepherders for a long time. Once here, once there, he tried to break out; but only with a hairline luck was he able to jump away from the heavily falling sticks; and he escaped already. The sheepherders cursed at his cunning style, but Runner's zigzags were performed out of fear and the skill set brought on by desperation. When the surrounding circle of men closed in, Runner made up his mind and started running with full power to where he saw less men in the circle's area. With a giant leap, he flew over the men's heads. The leaded stick caught him in the air, and Runner scrambled with his legs even in the snow, as if still trying to escape. Great Hunter soon realized that running here would not help him in this situation. He lay flat behind a big reed-bog and waited motionless. To lurk was much harder than running, when every muscle and part of your body wanted to escape. Great Hunter's body experienced a light shake running through him. His heart was shaking. It was almost impossible to hold himself down to the ground. He saw the long legs of the men pass by and felt their unpleasant smell and voice, but still did not move. Ultimately, one disobedient muscle could have been a giveaway, because one of the shepherds looked straight into Great Hunters eyes.

He screamed in his surprise. Great Hunter jumped up. It was too late. The shepherd's stick found his head in the air. "It's a wolf!" said the shepherd. He was very happy because he had been wanting a wolf skin for himself for a long time now. Without delay, he kneeled down to skin his wolf before its corpse got cold. He took out his knife and started to cut Great Hunter's belly. He reached half way when Great Hunter came to his senses from his stupor; he jumped up and with a staggering movement started running. "Hey!" shouted the shepherds. And they ran after Great Hunter. Everybody shouted all around and beat the wolf's trail with their sticks. With every passing second, Great Hunter grew conscious, and with his sure legs; his run became swifter. He was lucky since the sheepherders left the dogs to watch the sheep flocks. Their sticks were flying and whistling. One stick hit his leg. But even with three legs, he ran faster in the deep snow than the men who were after him. Great Hunter quickly vanished into the reeds. The sheepherders never saw Great Hunter again. They would not know if he perished or become part of the wolf packs. However, they said ten years later a big forest wolf showed up that looked just like Great Hunter.

There lied the one who escaped, and they turned their eyesight from the wolf, not looking so that the wolf would not bring trouble to them. Little One was left alive in the circle. She probably gave up her faith very quickly. She lay flat in the snow and was remorseful, imploring and whining; she crawled at the man's feet. She was not acting to be cunning: some deep affection and humility took grip over her, and a great consciousness— even she did not know the purpose for it. Yet, she felt it. The men were angry at them, and that was enough for Little One to prove her culpability.

She wagged her tale as she lay down. She would not raise herself, even when the men started to shout loudly after Great Hunter's escape. By chance, she was in front of the man who a few years back broke his leg. He raised his stick to kill Little One, but dropped his stick down.

"No. By God, you are a dog," he said and bent down to pat Little One on the head. And Little One happily rubbed the man's leg.

EPILOGUE

Little One lay next to the extension house, watching the sheep resting sheep flock. Around her were three large sized puppies jumping, whose father was the village's biggest kuvasz. Two of the puppies were almost snow-white, only a light gray color ran through on their backs. The third one looked like Great Hunter, a gray one. Little One rested her head on her stretched-out front legs as she watched the man sitting and talking around the fire. As the sheep flock stirred, the untamed reeds' nightly noises were at rest.

Once upon a time, two centuries ago; Hungary was covered with widespread far-reaching reeds and wild waters, especially at the south Ecsed swamp and the river Korosok.

The Transdanubian Sarret kept the land intact for a long time; the memory of the seas that had long disappeared, filled with wild game and fish. The humans, who in their gathering search for food settled down sporadically on the ancient, natural, undisturbed territory that over time gave safe haven to escaping peasants and virtuous poor young lads pressed by the law. In the great territory covered by the reeds and water; the lawman labanc (mixed soldiers, Austrian-Hungarian), Turkish, Tartar, or other invading forces could not find the hiding people who were running away to save their lives. The reeds offered concealment. Between the great big open waters, wheat fields existed. But, for the people of the reeds; the main source of food were live-stock farming and breeding. All the while, fishing and reed collecting brought an extra income to the household. A big part of the territories land was covered by water. Many times, two villages were so near to one another that a dog's bark was able to be heard from the short distance. And the people still had to go around with carriage for many miles if they wanted to go and reach the other village. Otherwise, those who lived in the reeds went around with barge. The reed was full of food. A bare hand was able to catch a fish— that is how many there were in the water. The reeds were a world of shepherds and refugees that lived in thatched huts. The huts were built on the kotu. The kotu was a bunch of reed roots anchoring the foundation of the huts, which was strong enough to carry a man's weight. The bigger kotu was never covered by water. Even the persecuted looked for cover in this area. The plot of this novel by Szasz Imre was played to the tune of this romantic, ancient, nomadic, preserved lifestyle that encapsulated a good deal of the Magyars' past. Today, you are able to find this fairy-tale land where Basa and her family lived a real, genuine, and strenuous life; only in traces.

www.ingramcontent.com/pod-product-compliance
Lightning Source LLC
Chambersburg PA
CBHW030815200726
48288CB00004B/1241